CW00519722

Tagore's Best Short Stories

Tagore's Best Short Stories

Translated from the Bengali by
Malobika Chaudhuri

With an introduction by
Patrick Colm Hogan

frontpage

frontpage

www.frontpagepublications.com

First published 2011

Frontpage Publications Limited
5 Percy Street, London W1T 1DG, United Kingdom

Frontpage
Level 6, Constantia, 11 Dr U N Brahmachari Sarani
Kolkata 700017, India

Copyright @ Publisher

All rights reserved. No part of this publication may be reproduced,
stored or introduced into a retrieval system, or transmitted, in
any form, or by any means (electronic, mechanical, photo-
copying, recording or otherwise) without the prior
written permission of the publisher. Any
person who does any unauthorised
act in relation to this publication
may be liable to criminal
prosecution and civil
claims for damages

ISBN 978 81 908841 5 0

Printed in India
By Sadhana Press Private Limited
76 B B Ganguly Street, Kolkata 700012, India

Contents

The selected short stories have been arranged according to the time of composition/publication. It mirrors the gradual progression of the Bard's mind through passage of time.

Introduction

Who Was Rabindranath Tagore?

The obvious place to begin an introduction to a collection of stories is with the identity of the author. But Tagore is a figure who defies categorisation or summary. The phrase "Renaissance man" was coined to refer to figures such as Leonardo da Vinci who excelled in a range of fields. But in scope of accomplishments, Tagore surpasses even such a paragon. Tagore wrote poetry, drama, novels, social and political treatises, philosophical and religious reflections; he was a painter and composer of music; he was an educator and a political activist. What is more remarkable still is that he excelled in all these areas on the global stage. The stature of Tagore's work is nowhere more clear than in his short stories, some of which are among the great treasures of world literature.

In keeping with the diversity of his genius, Tagore has been, so to speak, made into many different Tagores – some of them, to all appearances, mutually contradictory. There was the mystical Tagore, author of "Gitanjali". There was the rationalist Tagore who disagreed with Gandhi over whether a natural disaster (such as an earthquake killing many people) could be viewed as a punishment for communal sin. There was Tagore the nationalist, author of the Indian national anthem. There was Tagore the internationalist, famous for his powerful critique of nationalism.

Different Tagores have served different purposes in different times and places. The publication of a new, English translation of some of his stories, in commemoration of the 150th anniversary of his birth, raises the question of which Tagore is most significant today. More simply, it leads us to ask – how can a global readership in the twenty-first century understand and respond to an author born a century and a half ago in colonial India? Contrary to what this question suggests, it is possible that such a readership might understand Tagore better, more fully, than readers in the past. Removed from the pressing debates of the time, we may be in a better position now to acknowledge the diversity and scope of his thought, while at the same time recognising its deep coherence.

Tagore's Stories : The Morality of Feeling

Literature generally has two purposes – to affect the reader emotionally and to communicate some ethical, social, or related idea of the world outside the story. In principle, the two should work together. The emotion should motivate our response to the idea and the idea should guide the enactment of our feelings. Thus a work may inspire revulsion at the cruelty of war, or anger over the deprivations that result from colonialism. The point holds generally. But it is perhaps particularly salient in Tagore. For Tagore, politics and emotion are intertwined from the start because, for him, there is no ethics without feeling.

This is not to say that all emotions are equal for Tagore. Certainly, one finds a range of affect in his work. But there is one emotion that is particularly and distinctively pervasive in Tagore's writings. It is what psychologists refer to as "attachment," the bond that leads us to delight in the presence of another person, and makes separation painful; the bond that makes us wish to help, comfort, and cherish that person, and wish to be helped, comforted, and cherished by him or her. The prototype for such bonding is the relation of parents and small children. But we also feel attachment for spouses, siblings, friends.

Tagore enhances and generalises the relation of attachment – or *vatsalya*, as the Sanskrit aestheticians would have said. He often represents parents and children. But he also treats childhood friends, lovers, adults and children who are not biologically related (e.g., Raicharan and Khokababu in *"Khokababur Pratyabartan"*). Moreover, he integrates attachment with empathy. The two are already related, for attachment enhances the empathic connection between two people. But Tagore also develops the empathic aspects of attachment in order to extend the feeling of attachment to readers, allowing us to simulate and feel a character's joy over reunion or grief at loss.

Tagore is particularly concerned with developing empathy in two areas where that feeling is often inhibited. The first is in-group/out-group divisions. Research in social psychology presents ample evidence that we all tend to see ourselves as members of some groups – racial, religious, national, and so on. It also shows that we sharply distinguish between members of our in-group (e.g., our race or nation) and members of other groups. Empathic response is spontaneously inhibited across such groups. But Tagore is at pains to cultivate empathy across these group boundaries. He often does this precisely by appealing to the attachment relations of some character from an out-group (i.e., a national or other group different from that of his readers). *"Kabuliwallah"* presents a fine case of this in its portrayal of the Afghani father separated from his family.

Beyond this, Tagore recognised that, even outside group divisions, individuals come to be scapegoats. Sometimes a person has no support, no network of social defence, and ends up as the object of other people's aggression. Bindu in *"Streer Patra"* is a heartbreaking example. Here, too, Tagore cultivates empathy by stressing attachment, particularly Bindu's attachment to Mrinal.

As these examples suggest, Tagore's ethics are to a great extent based on empathy for others – scapegoats and out-group members – whom he humanised through relations of attachment. Other people are not simply abstract bearers of intellectually defined rights, or mere bodies that need food. Rather, we are all fundamentally caregivers and recipients of care – children and parents, spouses, friends, siblings. Perhaps the fundamental principle of Tagore's implicit ethics is that we should respect others as both subjects and objects of attachment. In relation to this, the inhibition of empathy and the rupturing of attachment bonds become perhaps the most fundamental and tragic sins.

These two emotional foci – attachment and empathy and their ethical associations are present across a range of Tagore's works. However, their affective force and thematic point are perhaps clearest in the short stories. Specifically, Tagore's stories frequently involve the development of some attachment relation, then its breaking apart. The break may result most directly from the foolishness or rashness of the main character. But it is typically underwritten by scapegoating or group division as well. Such division may be a matter of class, as at the end of "*Khokababur Pratyabartan*," or it may result from caste, religion, family or other categories.

Understanding the nature of empathy in Tagore's work helps us to understand some of what appear to be contradictions in his writing, for example his status as both a nationalist and an internationalist. Tagore's nationalism was anti-colonial. It derived from his preference for the underdog, whoever is downtrodden, scapegoated, and, thus, likely to lose other people's empathy. His internationalism derived from his opposition to divisions between in-groups and out-groups, which also serve to inhibit empathy.

Six Things to Look for in Reading Tagore

Needless to say, Tagore's treatments of attachment and empathy, as well as their limitations by group divisions and scapegoating, are manifest in multiple ways in the stories. Moreover, they are not the only components of those stories. Indeed, the stories are as multifaceted as the author himself. Yet they often seem terribly simple. That apparent simplicity can be misleading. For this reason, readers unfamiliar with Tagore may find it helpful to have a few key topics in mind when approaching the stories. Here is a brief list, stressing consequential and recurring points that contribute to the subdued complexity of the works.

1. *Historical and cultural particularity.* Tagore's stories are filled with the history of India, the philosophies of Vedantism and Buddhism, Hindu devotionalism, and other strains of Indian culture. For example, Krishnabhakti – love of the God Krishna and desire for union with him – is a recurring source of imagery and emotional resonance in Tagore's writings. A reader familiar with that tradition is likely to experience the culmination of "*Ek Ratri*" very differently from a reader who is not familiar with that tradition. In this way, reading Tagore's stories should repeatedly direct the reader to broader cultural and historical contexts.

2. *Generalisability.* But at the same time readers should be equally aware of the cross-cultural and trans-historical resonances of Tagore's stories. For example, in "*Streer Patra*," Bindu's disenfranchisement is bound up with the particular social and religious customs of Bengal at the period when the story was written. But her condition is almost identical with that of millions of refugees today. More generally still, it is a case of scapegoating with which all of us are undoubtedly familiar from family life, work, school, and elsewhere.

3. *Constraints on empathy imposed by abstract allegiances.* In "*Streer Patra*," Mrinal laments that human beings have not only hearts but also scriptures. The idea is that abstractions govern and suppress our human feelings, often with destructive consequences. The point bears not only on ancient patriarchal law texts. It holds equally for modern commitments to, for example, national politics (which sever ties of attachment in such stories as "*Nashtaneer*") or commitments to rationalism or theosophy (which divide the cousins in "*Khsudhita Pashan*").

4. *Constraints on empathy imposed by individual wilfulness.* Of course, not all movements of the heart are good. Sometimes emotion too inhibits empathy and attachment. This is particularly true

when there is no time for rational consideration, including the consideration required to imagine another person's point of view. Rashness of this sort shatters attachment relations in a number of Tagore's stories.

5.   *Dialectic.* As the reader has no doubt noticed, there is a degree of tension between numbers 1 and 2, as well as numbers 3 and 4. Indeed, they are, on the surface, contradictory. This is because the complexity of life is manifest in the complexity of Tagore's stories. Life encompasses diverse tendencies. As an author, it was Tagore's job to manifest that complex diversity. He did this through a sort of dialectical interplay of apparent opposites. An example may be found in his treatment of gender. In many stories, Tagore harshly criticised male domination. But in a number of places, he indicated that there is something like a matriarchal hierarchy alongside the more obvious patriarchy. In connection with this, he showed how women too – more precisely, women of a certain class and with a certain household position – have their own spheres of authority that may also be oppressive.

6.   *Voice.* One of the most striking ways in which Tagore's work manifests the diversity of life is through a diversity of voices, particularly those of narrators. "*Atithi*" is a nuanced, largely omniscient third-person narrative. "*Ek Ratri*" is a first-person reminiscence without any particular context. "*Streer Patra*" is first-person in a particular context – a letter from a wife to the husband she has left. "*Khsudhita Pashan*" is an intricate work with multiple narrators. The main story is told by a narrator who is imbedded in the frame story of another narrator; moreover, the embedded narrator introduces yet a third narrator, who proceeds to begin a third story – which is, in fact, never finished. This play of multiple voices is both engaging and significant. It helps to make palpable the multiplicity of human voices in the real world, voices too readily suppressed due to group divisions, scapegoating, and the resulting inhibitions of empathy.

This multiplicity of voices returns us from characters to readers. Again, the preceding topics are only suggestions that might help orient an initial reading of Tagore's stories, hopefully revealing some of their complexity. They are not an end in themselves. Ultimately, Tagore would not wish readers to simply accept his or anyone else's voice (certainly not that of some critic writing seventy years after his death). Rather, he would almost certainly wish readers to bring what he and his many characters are saying in connection with their own voices, their own worlds, their own lives. Indeed, without that interconnection between the work and the reader, literature has no emotional force, and no ethical or social point.

30 March 2010

PATRICK COLM HOGAN
Professor, Department of English
Programme in Comparative Literature
Cultural Studies and India Studies
University of Connecticut
Storrs, USA

Tagore Castle at Shilaidaha (Bangladesh): witness to the birth of a potpourri of short stories by Rabindranath Tagore

Atithi
(The Visitor)

Chapter 1

Motilal Babu, the zamindar of Kanthaley, was travelling accompanied by his family. At noon, anchoring near the banks of the river, preparations were underway for the midday meal when all of a sudden a Brahmin lad, of about fifteen-sixteen, came up and asked, "Babu, where are all of you going?"

Moti Babu answered, "To Kanthaley".

"On the way, could you put me down at Nandigaon?"

Assenting, the babu asked, "What's your name?"

"Tarapada."

The fair boy was extremely handsome. His large eyes and smiling visage spoke of a fresh softness. He sported a soiled loin cloth and his bare body remained completely unadorned. It was as if some artist had fashioned with great care a flawless and attractive physique. In some past birth, he could have been a young ascetic and thanks to uncompromising, unstinting meditation, all that was excessive had been whittled away from his body and the result was the bearing and demeanour of a true Brahmin.

Very affectionately Motilal Babu responded, "My dear, finish your bath, your meal will be of course here, with us".

Tarapada answered, "Just a moment," and, unhesitatingly joined in the preparations for cooking. Motilal Babu's cook was not from Bengal and not used to cutting and cooking fish with any degree of expertise; Tarapada took over from him and not only proved his culinary skills, but also some vegetarian dishes cooked with obvious habitual ease. The cooking complete, Tarapada bathed in the river and, clad in fresh clothes, with the sacred thread clearly visible, presented himself to Moti Babu.

Tarapada was taken inside the boat, where Moti Babu's wife and nine-year old daughter waited. Annapurna, Moti Babu's wife, was overwhelmed with fondness on seeing the fetching lad and thought to herself – 'Oh – whose child could he be, from where has he appeared – how is his mother able to stay away from him?'

In due course two wooden-seats were laid side by side for Moti Babu and the young boy. The boy was not a particularly voracious eater; Annapurna assumed from the scanty quantity Tarapada put away that he was feeling awkward. She repeatedly requested him to partake of this, that or the other. However, once he had stopped eating, nothing could change his mind. It was observed that the young boy strictly followed the norms he had set for himself; but he did so in such an easygoing manner that not a trace of stubbornness or obstinacy was to be found in his behaviour. Neither could any hint be found of embarrassment in his conduct.

After everyone had eaten, Annapurna seated the young boy close and attempted to glean some personal information from him. No details could be extracted. All that could be wrested was – at the young age of eight or nine, Tarapada, of his own volition, had run away from home.

Annapurna asked, "Don't you have a mother?"

"Yes, of course."

"Does she not love you?"

Considering on such a question as being quite absurd, Tarapada laughed aloud and answered, "Why would she not?"

Annapurna persisted, "Then why did you leave her and come away?"

"She has four more sons and three daughters."

Such a strange blasé attitude hurt Annapurna and she asked,

"What kind of a remark is that? If one has five fingers, does it mean one would cut-off and discard one?"

Tarapada was young and his past history proportionately sparse; but the youngster was of an absolutely new ilk. He was the fourth son of his parents and had been rendered fatherless at a very young age. Even in a household of many children, Tarapada was quite a favourite of all; his mother, the siblings and all the people in his locality would shower him love and affection. As a matter of fact, even the teachers refrained from berating him harshly. Under such circumstances, it was practically unthinkable for him to take flight from home. The thin emaciated boy who unrestrainedly and continually stole fruit from neighbouring trees and more than amply was beaten remained behind in the village with his tyrannical mother; but the adored son and child with no compunction whatsoever took to his heels with a foreign touring theatre company!

A search was immediately organised and Tarapada was hauled back home. His mother clasped him to her chest and drenched him with tears; Tarapada's sisters too wept copiously. His elder brother – stepping into the role of male guardian – made a half-hearted attempt to chide him, but finally regretfully stopped and compensated by fulsome indulgence and rewards. All the women of the locality invited him and not only overwhelmed him with love, but also alluring promises. But no bonds – even those of love – could restrain him. It was his stars that rendered him homeless. Whenever he espied boats from foreign climes on the river, or some sage from afar who had taken shelter beneath the towering shady tree in the village, or vagabonds setting up temporary shelter in the abandoned field along the river line, Tarapada's innermost being would be in a turmoil. He hankered for the loveless independence of the outside world. After two or three consecutive attempts at escape, his relatives and people of the village gave up all hopes for him.

At first, he had joined an itinerant theatre troupe. The leader of the group began to look on him as a son and yet again he came to be the favourite of all – from the elderly to the youngsters. But, as a matter of fact, when the head of the house where the plays were staged, especially the women of the household began to ask after him and indulge him, suddenly, without telling a soul, he disappeared and could not be found.

Tarapada was chary about being tethered – just like an untrammelled fawn. And, further, the young lad was characteristically partial to music. It was the predilection for melody that first tore asunder his ties with his home. The strains of a song would make his nerves quiver and the rhythmic beat of any song would cause his entire body to shiver. When he was little more than an infant, the grave and engrossed manner in which he conducted himself at any musical soirée made restraining their laughter a tough task for the elderly people. Not only music – when rain poured down torrentially on the lush green trees, and thunder resounded in the sky and the wind shrieked and cried like an orphaned giant child in the forests, Tarapada's innermost being was thrilled in frenzy. Everything – from the shrill call of eagles in the boundless sky on a still afternoon, the noisy croaking of frogs on a rainy monsoon evening, the baying of foxes at the dead of night – all this evoked violent restlessness in him. It was this magnetic pull for music which made him join a musical troupe and the members with great care began to teach him the niceties and nitty-gritty of their genre of music. Like their own favourite bird, they taught him to sing in the manner they knew best. The bird learnt for a while and early one morning took flight for climes unknown.

The last time he had joined a gymnastics troupe. From the beginning of summer to almost the end of the rainy season, a number of fairs took place all around and a number of specialities were seen. The previous year a small gymnastics troupe from Kolkata had happened to join the activities and merriment. Tarapada had joined hands with the owner of the first boat and had engaged himself in selling betel leaves. Later, a sense of marvel and curiosity in the skill and adroitness of gymnastics had incited him into joining them. By dint of his own practice, Tarapada had become quite skilled in playing the flute. His only job was to play the flute to a very fast beat when the show was on.

The escapade from this troupe was his last. He had heard that the zamindars of Nandigram were starting an amateur theatre troupe with a lot of fanfare. Hearing this, he had readied his small bundle of belongings and was getting ready to leave when he came across Moti Babu and his family.

Thereafter, despite mingling with various troupes, Tarapada's naturally imaginative nature was not particularly influenced by any of them. He remained detached and free. There was a lot of ugliness in life that he had seen and even more ugliness that he had heard of. But, none of the dark degenerations he witnessed made any impact on him. This boy had no mind to anything. Neither was there any habit which held him in its coils. Life to him was like turbid waters in which he moved about regally like a pristine white swan. Out of curiosity, no matter how many times he took a quick dip, nothing sullied him. That was probably why this runaway shone with an unspoiled natural youth; it was that visage that had led the elderly worldly Moti Babu to welcome him affectionately, and without any suspicion or questions.

Chapter 2

At the end of the meal, the ferry set sail. With a great deal of affection, Annapurna began to question this Brahmin lad about his home and relatives. Somehow Tarapada escaped the tirade after some extremely terse replies. Outside, the monsoon river in full spate, overflowing to the last line of demarcation, remained self-engrossed in frenzied preoccupation, causing Mother Nature grave concern. In the cloudless sunlight by the riverside, half submerged grass flowers and the bamboo shoots and, further beyond, the boundary line of the forest... Like the fresh beauty awakened by the magical golden wand of some fairytale, beneath the mesmerised mute glance of the blue sky all had come to life; all appeared wondrously alive, pulsating, flooded with a kind of ethereal light and polished and glistening – replete in plenty.

Tarapada took shelter on the roof of the ferry. As the boat moved along, progressively – lush green expanses, flooded jute fields, deep green paddy fields, narrow paths leading from the ferry jetty towards the village and the village surrounded by thick shadowy forest all passed before his eyes – water all around, land, sky and vibrancy in the air. But there was no effort at all to hold this restless being in bonds of affection. On the river banks calves ran about, village horses champed – the grass – all these familiar and yet novel sights Tarapada thirstily imbibed; there was no quenching – his passion for open nature.

Reaching the roof, Tarapada set up a conversation with the boatman and all his companions. As need arose, sometimes he voluntarily took up the oars from them and enthusiastically tried his hand at steering! Whenever the helmsman required taking a puff, he adroitly took over his task.

Before evening Annapurna sent for Tarapada and asked, "What is your normal fare in the evening?"

"Whatever is available and sometimes nothing at all..."

The indifference of this Brahmin lad in accepting their hospitality began to trouble Annapurna. She keenly desired that by dint of feeding and clothing him, this run away from home would be made replete. In no way, however, she could gauge just what would satisfy him. Annapurna set up a hue and cry about sending servants to purchase sweets and milk. Tarapada graciously partook of them, but refused the milk. The generally taciturn Moti Babu also added his request, but the young boy abruptly replied, "I do not like it".

Two or three days passed on the river. Tarapada willingly participated in all activities – cooking, marketing or steering the boat. Whatever scene passed before his eyes, curiously he went in pursuit; whatever task befell – involuntarily he was attracted. His vision, hands and mind always remained active. That is probably why, like the eternally active Nature, he too remained passively uninvolved and yet always active. As a human, every individual has his own demarcated zone; but Tarapada remained outside the purview of it all. He appeared to have no links with the past or the future – he was only part of what was taking place at the moment.

Presently, having been involved with many troupes and organisations Tarapada was well-versed in the art of entertainment. Not being clouded with any mundane issues, he had a startling clear memory which could easily retain whatever and whenever required. Mythological stories, religious incantations or songs – he was well-versed in them all. One evening, as was his practice, Moti Babu was reading aloud from the religious text, the Ramayana. Unable to restrain his excitement Tarapada rapidly descended from the roof and asked Moti Babu to shut the book as he would sing aloud the verses from memory.

In a sweet and lilting voice the boy began – all listened mesmerised. All aboard stopped work and peered in through the door; an indescribable mingling of laughter, tragedy and melody resounded that evening on that serene and tranquil corner of the river. The silent banks on both sides resounded with curiosity, passengers in all the boats that passed by for a few seconds gazed with unabashed inquisitiveness and tried to take in what was being recited. When the impromptu soirée finally came to an end, all sighed unhappily, wondering – why did it have to end so soon.

The tearful Annapurna Devi wished that she could clasp him to her bosom and inhale his fragrance. Moti Babu began to ponder, 'If somehow this boy can be kept in close proximity, my hunger for a son will be fulfilled'. It was only the little girl Charusashi whose heart brimmed over with an acute envy and hatred.

Chapter 3

Charusashi was the only child of her parents and hence the only one privy to all their parental love and affection. She was not only whimsical, but extremely stubborn as well. The young girl had very strong opinions about her mode of dressing and attire, but there was no firmness associated with those opinions. Should there be any invitation, her mother would be tense in case she came up with some absurd demand which would be well nigh impossible to meet. If unfortunately her tresses were not dressed right the first time, no matter how many times opened and re-done, it would be impossible to gain her approval. The final and only outcome would be an abundance of tears. It was the same in everything else. On the other hand, when she was content and happy, she would not object to anything at all. Then, with an excessive show of love, she would embrace her mother and shower her with kisses and affection amidst laughter and smiles. This small girl was truly an enigma.

Projecting all the force of her incomprehensible heart, this child began to hound Tarapada with an intense hatred. Even her parents were not spared. In a flood of tears she would push away her food during meal, nothing that was cooked could please her, she would hit out at the servants all the time and for no reason at all there would be a continual volley of complaints. As Tarapada grew more adept at entertaining her and all the others, his popularity proportionately grew greater. It went absolutely against the grain for her to even acknowledge that Tarapada had any praiseworthy qualities; however, when there was undeniable proof of all his virtues, her acute ennui spiralled upwards even more. The day Tarapada sang aloud from the scriptures Annapurna thought to herself, 'After all, music tames even wild animals – perhaps my daughter will be appeased at long last'. She ventured to ask, "Charu, how did you find this?" The girl made no answer, except to violently shake her head. If the gesture were to be analysed through the medium of language, the meaning would stand as – not a jolt of it was to taste and neither was there any chance of any favourable impression being made on her any time in the future.

Realising that Tarapada provoked strong feelings of jealousy, Annapurna refrained from any public display of affection for Tarapada in her daughter's presence. Fairly early in the evening, when Charu would retire for the day after her meal, Annapurna Devi would sit at the threshold of the door; with Moti Babu and Tarapada sitting outside, she would request Tarapada to begin singing. When the restful rustic silence of the river banks in the overwhelming darkness remained in stupefied calm and Annapurna's tender heart overflowed with affection and a sense of beauty, suddenly Charu would descend on them like a whirlwind. Angrily and brimming over with tears she would complain, "Mother, what kind of furore have all of you set up – I cannot sleep". It was impossible for her to tolerate the fact that sending her to sleep alone, her parents were enjoying Tarapada's company.

In turn Tarapada felt a strange curiosity for this bright, determined and vibrant young girl. Through narrating stories, singing songs, playing the flute he wasted no effort in overcoming her resistance – but to no avail. It was only at midday, when Tarapada went to swim in the river, she could not resist the fascination of the easy manner in which the healthy young lad frolicked in the water. She would wait impatiently for such a time, but let none know of this attraction. Apparently engrossed in knitting Charu would once in a while cast covert glances at the lad swimming in the water.

Chapter 4

When Nandigaon passed by, Tarapada made no movement or enquiry. The large boat moved sedately, sometimes with sails raised along the various tributaries of the river. Similarly, the days for all aboard – like the river and its tributaries – went by in beauteous diversity in easy gait and mild clamour. None was in any hurry; the midday meal was a leisurely and delayed affair. On the other hand, as evening fell, the boat would be anchored beside the river banks of a large village, amidst the pleasant verdant ambience of a forest.

In this manner, Kanthaley was reached in about ten days. At the advent of the zamindar, palanquins and horses were organised. Well – armed escorts firing blankly into the air and setting up an anxious furore amongst the crow community wound their way to their destination.

All these momentous events taking time, Tarapada rapidly descended from the boat and took a rapid survey of the village. Addressing all he met as some relative or the other, in a very short while the lad found a niche for himself in the heart of the entire village community. The very fact that he truly had no bonds at all led the young boy with astounding ease and rapidity to establish an acquaintance with all.

The reason behind so easily winning the hearts of all was simply that Tarapada mixed with all at their level and in the manner to which they were accustomed. He was not shackled by any particular convention – but he retained an abundant enthusiasm in all circumstances and in every situation. To a young boy he was simply a lad like them and yet completely individualistic and superior to them, he was no child to the elderly and yet disgustingly over-mature, to a cowherd he was of their ilk and, despite being a Brahmin, Tarapada would participate and intervene in the affairs of all like their ever – familiar compatriot. At the local sweetmeat shop, the owner would call out, "Dadathakur, just stay here for a while – I'll be back very soon". Tarapada would happily sit there swatting flies. He had a smattering knowledge of various skills and was reasonably skilled in them.

Tarapada conquered the entire village, but it was only the resentment of one little girl that he just could not overcome. Probably it was because he knew how ardently she craved his banishment too far off climes that he remained in the village for such a long while.

Even as a child Charusashi proved that it is well nigh impossible to gauge the heart of a woman.

Sonamoni, Bamunthakurun's daughter, had been widowed at five; she was the closest to Charu in age. Not keeping well, she had been unable to meet her friend who only recently returned home. On her recovery, the day she came to meet Charu an irreparable quarrel all but tore both friends asunder.

Charu with a lot of fanfare had started on an elaborate tale. She had assumed that a detailed description of the advent of the new arrival of Tarapada would stimulate her friend's curiosity and stun her with amazement. However, she came to learn from her friend that Tarapada was no stranger to them, rather, he was on very familiar terms. She was further told that not only had her parents been entertained with musical soirées, but on Sonamoni's request he had also fashioned a flute from bamboo reeds for her. Further, he had also gathered flowers for her many a day. All these tales stung and lacerated her with pain. Charu had taken for granted that Tarapada was their sole. Tarapada – he was a secret treasure to be viewed guardedly from a distance by people in general, but would definitely have no access to him. They would marvel at his looks and admire his qualities from afar and repeatedly thank Charusashi and her family. Why had this astounding, divinely obtained Brahmin lad been so easily accessible? If we had not brought him here with so much care, tended to him so painstakingly – how would Sonamoni have caught sight of him? Now he was Sonamoni's brother! She fumed in rage.

Why such turbulent emotions centring on sole proprietorship over Tarapada – someone Charu had tried from her innermost being to shred into smithereens of hatred? Who was to understand the reason behind!

That very day, using a most trivial pretext as a cause, Sonamoni and Charu stopped all conversation and interaction with each other. Charu then marched to Tarapada's room and, finding his precious flute, broke it into tiny shreds.

When Charu was obsessively engaged in this wanton destruction, all of a sudden Tarapada entered the room. He was amazed at seeing this veritable tornado and asked, "Charu, why are you breaking my flute?" With bloodshot eyes scarlet faced Charu retorted, "Serves you right – I am glad," and after unnecessarily kicking the flute a couple of time and weeping copiously all the while she rushed out of the room. Picking up the offending article Tarapada found that nothing was left of it. He could not contain his laughter at seeing the sorry plight of his old and favourite flute.

Each and every single day Charusashi became an object of insatiable curiosity for him.

Another point of interest and curiosity for him were the books on English paintings in Moti Babu's library. Tarapada was quite familiar with the outside world, but somehow was just not able to forge an entry into the world of paintings. Thanks to an extremely active imagination, he compensated himself somewhat, but somehow just could not find true satisfaction.

Observing Tarapada's avid interest in paintings, Moti Babu one day asked him, "Do you want to learn English? You will then be able to understand the meaning of everything in the paintings". Tarapada instantly agreed.

Very pleased Moti Babu then arranged for Ramratan Babu, the Headmaster of the Village Entrance School, to teach this lad English every evening.

Chapter 5

Tarapada thus began his English lessons, depending on his razor sharp memory and focused concentration. It was as though he had begun traversing through a remote, new kingdom – there remained no further connection with his old world. The people of the locality no longer saw him all around. In the evening, as he strolled rapidly along the river banks, focusing on learning his lessons by rote, the young lads who looked on him reverently would gaze at him with awe but none dared disturb him as he studied.

Charu too could barely see him. Previously Tarapada used to eat in the inner sanctum, under the watchful and affectionate care of Annapurna. However, because there would be an ensuing delay, Tarapada spoke to Moti Babu and other arrangements were made outside. Annapurna was a little upset at this and objected; Moti Babu, greatly pleased with the boy's enthusiasm, however, consented to the new schedule.

All of a sudden Charu too stubbornly demanded, "I too want to learn English". Initially her parents treated this as yet another absurd notion of their whimsical daughter and laughed indulgently, but the laughter was shortly set awash by their child's shower of tears. Finally, this affectionately weak couple was forced into taking their daughter's demand seriously. Charu began her lessons along with Tarapada under the tutelage of the Headmaster.

Studying seriously did not come naturally to the restless girl. She did not learn anything herself, instead persistently disturbed Tarapada. She would fall back, not work on the homework set – but adamantly refused to follow Tarapada in any manner. If Tarapada superseded her and attempted to go on to a new lesson, she would throw tantrums and did not stop short of copious tears. If Tarapada completed his books and new ones were bought, a new set also had to be bought for her. The envious girl could not tolerate the fact that during his leisure hours Tarapada would sit in his room and work on his lessons; in secret she would ensure ink was dropped all over his writing, his pen would be stolen and she would also tar the pages of the book from which lessons had to be prepared. Tarapada would tolerate all the tyranny with affectionate indulgence and, when it became intolerable, would smack her, but just could not manage to control her.

All of a sudden a solution suddenly presented itself. One day the dejected Tarapada – greatly irritated with tearing and throwing away his ink sodden books – was sitting alone; Charu coming to the door assumed that she would definitely get a beating. However, her expectations did not transpire. Tarapada did not speak a word and remained in absolute silence. The girl began to hover all around; she came so close that Tarapada could easily have reached out and given her a blow on the back, but instead he remained gravely silent. The girl was in an absolute quandary. She had never been particularly adept in the art of apologising; at the same time her tender young heart desperately sought her co-student's forgiveness. Finally, not seeing any other alternative, she picked up a shred of the copy and wrote on it in big bold letters, I WILL NEVER EVER MESS YOUR COPY. She then restlessly began to try and draw his attention to the notice in a series of restless movements. Tarapada could no longer control himself and burst out laughing. In rage and embarrassment the girl rapidly ran out of the room. If she could only have for all time and from the entire universe eradicated the humiliating emotions expressed therein, the searing regret of her heart would have known relief.

Sonamoni had for a couple of days peeped into the classroom and surreptitiously tiptoed away. She was on the best of terms with her friend Charusashi in every respect except for matters regarding Tarapada; in this instance, Sonamoni would look on her with fear and the gravest of suspicions. At a time when she was confident that Charu would be in the inner sanctum would she go with great trepidation to Tarapada's door. He would look up from his books and with extreme affection say, "So Sona, what is happening? How is my aunt?"

"You have not come over for a number of days; mother has asked you to go over some time. Her hip is giving trouble and hence she cannot come."

At such a juncture Charu would sometimes suddenly appear. Sonamoni would be thrown into a frenzy of panic – as though she was secretively trying to usurp her friend's property. Distorting her face and in a high pitched voice Charu would shrilly cry out, "What, Sona! You have come here to cause problems during the study time. I will immediately complain to father". One had the impression that she was Tarapada's senior and guardian; her only task was to ensure that at no hour of the day or night any disturbance was caused to his studies. But the purpose with which she herself had gone to his room at that hour did not remain unknown to the Almighty and Tarapada too was well aware of the situation. However, the timid Sonamoni in fright would present a whole tissue of lies; finally when she would be castigated as a liar, vanquished, ashamed and humiliated Sona would leave. The tender hearted Tarapada would call out, "Sona, I will come by your place today evening". Like a wounded serpent Charu would lash out, "Definitely not! Don't you have studies to prepare? Won't I complain to our teacher?"

Not in the least intimidated by Charu's threats, Tarapada had gone across to Bamunthakurun's place once or twice in the evenings. The third or fourth time Charu made no further empty threats! She stealthily locked the door of Tarapada's room from the outside, hid the key in her mother's spice box – opening the door only when it was time for dinner. Enraged, Tarapada refused to eat and was about to leave when the repentant young girl wringing her hands began to repeatedly plead, "I implore you, never will I do this again. I beg of you to please have your meal". When even that did not melt the ice, Charu began to weep copiously. Feeling trapped, Tarapada sat down to eat.

Charu had solemnly promised innumerable times that she would behave well with Tarapada, not for an instant would she disturb him; but when Sonamoni and others turned up, her manner and intentions changed so diametrically that to retain any kind of control was virtually impossible. When for a prolonged consecutive period she would remain moderately gentle with decorum, Tarapada would remain tense and alert for some momentous and disastrous calamity. It was practically impossible to predict the reason for the furore or from which direction the attack would come. There would be a tumultuous storm followed by a torrential downpour of tears and, at the end, calm, peaceful tranquillity.

Chapter 6

Almost two years went by in this manner. Tarapada had never allowed himself to be tethered for such a long period anywhere. Perhaps the magnetic appeal of studies and education had succeeded in anchoring him. May be, with age, his innate nature was changing to some extent – his mind was gradually veering towards savouring the richness and bounty of life. Possibly the appeal behind his co-student's daily tyrannical mischief unknowingly had created strands of attachment.

With the passing of time, Charu was almost eleven years. Moti Babu, by dint of earnest looking around, located two or three promising matches for his daughter. Aware that his daughter had reached a marriageable age, Moti Babu stopped her English lessons and forbid her to step out of the house. At this sudden embargo Charu practically set up a revolt of sorts in the house.

One day Annapurna spoke to Moti Babu, "Why are you searching so assiduously for a suitor? Tarapada seems to be a fine lad and your daughter too has taken quite a liking to him".

Moti Babu was amazed, "How can that be possible! Nothing is known of his family and background. Charu is my only daughter – I want to marry her into a good family".

A family from Raidanga came to take a look at Charu, the proposed bride. Attempts were made to dress Charu and present her to the groom and his family. She locked the door of her room and refused to emerge. From outside Moti Babu entreated and chided her in no uncertain terms – but to no avail. Finally, he had no recourse but to lie and save face; he said that his daughter had suddenly taken ill and it was impossible for her to be brought out; the guests, however, assumed that there must be some marked flaw in the girl, which was why such an excuse was being presented.

Moti Babu then began to think, 'Tarapada is quite a handsome and presentable boy in every respect. We will be able to keep him at home and my only daughter will not have to be sent to her in-law's house. He also pondered on the fact that no matter how indulgently they might condone his unruly disobedient daughter, it would probably not be so forgivable in any in-law's home.

After consulting at length with his wife, messengers were sent to Tarapada's native village to find out about his religious and family background. The news came back to them that his family was not well off, but otherwise there was nothing objectionable. A marriage proposal was then sent to the boy's mother and brother. In euphoric joy, they lost no time at all in intimating their acceptance.

In Kanthaley, Moti Babu and Annapurna began to discuss wedding dates. But the naturally secretive Moti Babu chose to be very guarded about these plans.

Charu could not be restrained. Like a virtual marauder, she would sometimes raid Tarapada's room. Through rage, love, ennui – she would stir up a whirlwind. Thus these days, even the uninvolved free Brahmin lad would for just a few seconds be caught unawares and feel a lightening flash of some strange and sweet emotion. One who had all this while remained impassive and totally free of being buffeted by any emotion, sometimes grew absentminded and enmeshed in some mesmeric daydream. Some evenings, he would even discard his studies and entering Moti Babu's library turn the pages of all the books on paintings; the spell that was woven around them and the hazy dreams that resulted were far different and much more colourful than in the past. Taking note of Charu's strange behaviour, he found it impossible to behave normally; when she misbehaved, he found it unthinkable to smack her. This deep-rooted change in himself, this enmeshment of emotions, appeared as a strange new dream to his own self.

Fixing a day in the month of *Shravana* for the marriage to be solemnised, Moti Babu sent for Tarapada's mother and brothers, not, however, giving any inkling to Tarapada. Arrangements were also made as regards decorations and marriage after related fanfare.

Clouds heralding the arrival of the rainy season began to overcast the sky. The village which had been dry and had little more than a scanty flow of water suddenly overflowed the banks. All the village lads in glee and joyous merriment began to prance about and dive in and out of the puddles and ponds. A variety of boats, small and large, laden with goods of all kinds began to ply on the river; in the evenings the river banks began to resound with the melody of foreign boatmen. Villages located on either side lived and reined in solitary splendour and isolation through the year; but it was during the rainy season that the outside world with its abundance of diverse goods arrived via the watery pathway. For a short while, establishment of a relationship with the world momentarily eradicated their pettiness and all became living and vibrant and a silent sullen kingdom resounded all around with joyous laughter.

At about this time, in Kudulkata, at landlord Nag Babu's area, a popular fair took place. In the evening Tarapada went across to the landing jetty and noticed some boats laden with Ferris wheels, merry-go-rounds and various other means of entertainment – all moving rapidly with the current in the direction of the fair. The concert troupe from Kolkata had organised loud blaring music, the itinerant theatre group was singing to the accompaniment of a musical instrument – and in short the entire surrounding resounded with raucous merriment and enjoyment. In no time thick dark clouds appeared to sail into the centre of the sky, the moon was overshadowed – from the east a violent wind began to blow; clouds chased after clouds, the waters of the river bubbled in merriment and began to swell rapidly and grow turbid. The forests along the river banks grew overcast with an even thicker darkness, the croaking of frogs began to be heard and the sound of crickets sawed through the darkness... Presently the entire world appeared to be a gigantic fairground – wheels turned around, flags fluttered wildly, the universe trembled; in no time at all clouds violently sounded, flashes of lightning streaked across the sky, tearing it asunder, from the faraway darkness the fragrance of a torrential downpour wafted across. It was just only on one bank of the river, on the dormant other bank, the village of Kanthaley barred its doors and, blowing out lamps, surrendered to sleep.

The next day Tarapada's mother and brother descended at Kanthaley and boats laden with goods for the wedding began to anchor at the landing jetty.

One morning Sonamoni very timorously and surreptitiously stood at the entrance to Tarapada's study room – but from the next day Tarapada could not be found. Before the petty bonds of affection, love and friendship could completely enmesh him, carrying away the heart of the entire village, on a dark and rainy overcast monsoon night, this Brahmin lad had gone into the arms of the detached, impassive universal mother.

Dena Paona
(Debts and Dues)

After the birth of five sons, when a daughter was born, both parents lovingly named her Nirupama. None of the clan had ever heard of such a fancy name before. It was the name of deities that had been in vogue – prime examples of Ganesh, Kartik and Parvarti etc.

Presently marriage proposals were being sought for Nirupama. Her father Ramsunder Mitra sought far and wide, but no suitable groom was to be found. Finally, the only heir of a prosperous landed gentry was located. Though land and material assets of the said family were not as prolific as in the past, they were truly, blue-blooded.

The groom demanded as dowry a lot of money and expensive articles as gifts. Not giving the matter another thought, Ramsunder agreed; such a groom could not be allowed to go free under any circumstance.

It became practically impossible to gather the money. Despite mortgaging, selling and taking recourse to practically every option, still a substantial amount remained due. On the other hand, the wedding gradually drew near.

Finally it was the day of the marriage. There being no other option, some kind soul, charging an excessive rate of interest, had agreed to loan the remaining amount of money, but could not put in an appearance in time. An awful furore and chaos developed at the wedding site. Ramsunder practically went down on his hands and knees to the aforesaid gentry and pleaded, "Let the auspicious task go through without a hitch – all my debts will definitely be paid".

At this disaster there was a plethora of tears in the inner sanctum. The core of all this problem sat dressed in all her wedding finery – quiet and downcast. It could definitely not be said that feelings of devotion and love for her to be in-laws were in any way growing.

In the meanwhile, there was some resolution. The groom suddenly turned disobedient. He addressed his father, "I do not understand all this haggling about money and the like; I have come here to marry and will do so".

The father told whoever would listen, "What can you possibly say about the behaviour of children of this generation?" Some venerable elderly people around commented, "There is no education in the scriptures or traditional norms – what else can be expected!"

Observing the evils of modern education in his own son the gentleman remained in a dumbstruck stupor. The marriage took place albeit – in a somewhat gloomy and depressed ambience.

Just before Nirupama journeyed to her in-law's house, her father drew her close and could no longer check his tears. Niru asked, "Then, father, will they no longer permit me to visit you?" Ramsunder answered, "Why not my dear, I myself will go to fetch you".

Ramsunder frequently visited his daughter, but no great respect was shown to him there. Even the servants looked down on him. In a room adjacent to the inner sanctum, sometimes he would be permitted to see his daughter for a couple of minutes and sometimes not.

Such insult could no longer be tolerated. Ramsunder decided that somehow or the other the money would have to be repaid.

But the burden that the debt had placed on him was not easy to shrug off. Expenses kept mounting and, in order to avoid his creditors, he was forced to take recourse to various lowdown tactics.

Nirupama too had to contend with innumerable barbs from her in-laws. It became a regular practice for her to be reviled with abuses regarding her father and weep after locking her room.

Particularly it was her mother-in-law who just could not keep control on her rage. "What beauty, just to look at the bride's face is mesmerising!" – if any commented thus, the mother-in-law would flare up, "What looks! She is just as her background suggests".

Even as regards meals, no attention was paid to what Nirupama partook of. If some kindly neighbour made a reference to some fault, the retort promptly came, "That is more than enough". The inherent message behind this was – if the entire sum of money had been paid, Nirupama would have been well looked after. All gave to understand that the bride had no true rights in the house – she had slipped in using some kind of trickery.

Probably all the humiliation and insult his daughter was facing reached her father's ears. So, Ramsunder began to try and sell his ancestral house.

However, he kept it a secret from his sons that he was on the verge of making them homeless. He had decided that after selling his house, he would continue to live there – paying rent. Ramsunder would conduct matters in such a way that till moments before his death none would be able to make out the true situation.

But his sons did learn the facts and came to him, weeping. Particularly affected were his three elder sons – some of whom even had children of their own. Their objections assumed serious proportions and the sale of the house was put-off.

Then, Ramsunder began to borrow small amounts of money at inordinately high rates of interest. Matters came to such a pass that it became virtually impossible to meet household expenses.

Looking at her father, it was only too apparent to Niru what was happening. The careworn old man's white hair, wan demeanour, permanently apologetic manner all spoke loudly of poverty and an overriding worry. When a father had done his daughter an injustice, could it possibly be hidden from her? When Ramsunder somehow managed to see his daughter for a couple of minutes with her in - laws' reluctant permission, the agony that her father went through was only too apparent from his smile.

In order to soothe that hurt at least a little, Niru became desperate to go and spend a few days with her father. It was impossible for her to remain at a distance seeing her father's washed out face. One day she told Ramsunder, "Father, take me home for a few days". "Alright" was the response.

But, Ramsunder had no voice or authority at all; the natural right that a father had over his daughter appeared to have been mortgaged in lieu of the promised dowry money. Even the favour of seeing his daughter was sought in an apologetic and servile manner and sometimes – when rejected there was no opportunity to say even another word.

How was it possible for a father to ignore his daughter's plea when she wanted to come home? Thus, before supplicating his daughter's father-in-law, it might be better not to reveal the degree of humiliation, insult and injury Ramsunder had to face in order to gather three thousand rupees.

Wrapping the notes in a handkerchief and carefully tying it to one end of his shawl, Ramsunder reached his destination. He began the proceedings by smilingly bringing up all the news of the locality. Mention was made of the theft in Harekrishna's house; then, reference was Nabinmadhab and Radhamadhab – two brothers' qualifications and otherwise. Ramsunder also discussed some new disease that was doing its round of the city, and all the ensuing absurdities. Then, in the course of conversation, Ramsunder casually mentioned – "Oh yes, each day when I come over, I must bring along some part of the money that still remains dues. But, then, it is impossible to remember everything all the time. All said and done, I am getting old after all". After such a lengthy introduction, very casually he brought out and handed over the three heart-rending currency notes.

Noting that the amount was only three thousand rupees Raibahadur burst out laughing. He said, "Never mind, don't bother about that sum of money any longer". He drove home the fact with the help of a proverb that, there was no vestige of desire in him to thus sully his hands.

After such an incident it was unseemly for anyone to bring up the topic of getting the daughter home – however, Ramsunder thought to himself, 'It does not suit me to nurture such delicacy'. After maintaining a hurt silence for a while, hesitantly he brought up the subject. Not giving any reason at all, Raibahadur abruptly getting up said, "No, that is impossible at the moment".

Not waiting to meet his daughter Ramsunder once again tied up the notes and left the place. Firmly he resolved to himself – till such a time that he could repay the entire amount of money and re-establish the natural rights of a father over his daughter, he would no longer go across to meet his daughter.

A number of days went by; Nirupama sent innumerable messages through people, but her father still remained out of touch. Finally, hurt, she stopped communicating. Though that greatly upset Ramsunder, he still did not go across.

The month of Aswin came around and Ramsunder said, "During the festivities of this Puja, I will definitely get my daughter home or else ..." – he made a very harsh resolution to himself.

Just before the Pujas, once again wrapping a few notes into a handkerchief Ramsunder made preparations for the journey. His five year old grandson came up and asked, "Dada, are you going to buy a car for me?" Since a very long time he had been nurturing a desire to go for a ride on such a vehicle, but somehow that was just not happening. A six year old grand-daughter came up with the complaint that she didn't have any Puja clothes at all to go visiting during the festive season.

Ramsunder was well aware of that and while puffing away on the hookah, had pondered on the matter long and hard. When an invitation would come from the Raibahadur, it would have to be accepted and he would also have to incur further humiliation. All these thought made him sigh deeply. However, the only effect was to etch even deeper lines of worry on his forehead.

The cries of his poverty-stricken family resounding in his ears, Ramsunder entered the house of his daughter's in-laws. No longer did he have the careworn, embarrassed and awkward demeanour and nor did he cast an apologetic look at the guards. Ramsunder strode in as though it were his own house. He was informed that Raibahadur was not at home and he would have to wait for some time. Unable to control the effusive joy in his heart, Ramsunder met his daughter and started weeping in joy. The tears of both father and daughter flowed freely and none could speak. Some time went by in this manner. At last Ramsunder spoke, "Now, I will take you home, my child – there are no more barriers."

All of a sudden Ramsunder's elder son with his two sons in tow entered the room, "Father, have you thrown us to the wolves in this manner?" Ramsunder flared up, "Will I then go to hell because of you all? Will you not let me pursue my path of truth?" Ramsunder had sold the house and gone to a lot of trouble to ensure that his sons did not come to know. Despite it, the fact that they had come to know angered and irritated him no end.

His grandson clung forcibly to his knees and looking up said, "Dada, did you not buy a car for me?"

Not getting a suitable response from him, the child then turned to Niru and said, "Aunt, will you at least buy me a car?"

The entire matter being clear to Nirupama, she turned to her father, "I swear in your name that if you give my father-in-law even one rupee more, you will never ever see your daughter again".

Ramsunder responded, "Shame on you my dear, you must not talk in this manner. If this money is not repaid, it is an insult to your father and to you".

Niru answered, "It is an insult only if you hand over the money. Does your daughter have no honour at all? Am I just a money-making machine that I am held in regard only when I can draw in money and not otherwise? Besides, my husband does not want this money. No, father, you must not insult me by giving more money".

Ramsunder persisted, "But then they will not permit you to leave".

Nirupama answered, "In that case there is nothing further to be done. You need not try to persuade them any longer".

With trembling finger, Ramsunder once again picked up the bundle of notes wrapped in cloth and, evading all glances, left the house.

However, that Ramsunder had brought along the money and because of his daughter had left without handing it over did not remain a secret. Some verbose, curious maid gave Niru's mother-in-law this bit of information. Her enraged fury knew no bounds.

Nirupama's home became a living hell for her. Her husband had been posted far away as the District Magistrate very shortly after marriage. Using the pretext of keeping her safe and secure from malicious gossip, all contact with Niru's paternal relatives had been stopped.

At about this time Niru fell grievously ill. But her mother-in-law could not really be faulted in this instance. Niru was very negligent as regards her own health. Through the chilly winter months she would sleep with the windows open and wear no warm clothes at all. Niru had extremely irregular eating habits. If the maids sometimes forgot to bring her food, she would not even bother to call out and remind them. The belief had become ingrained in her that she was living in that household dependent on the charity of the maid- servants and her in-laws. This attitude too made her mother-in-law fly into a fury. If any ennui was observed as regards her eating, her mother-in-law would scathingly comment – "After all, belonging to such aristocracy, such poor fare does not interest her". Sometimes the comment would be "Look at her – no better than a living skeleton".

When the sickness assumed serious proportions, her mother-in-law said, "All this is mere playacting". Finally, one day, Niru said in all humility, "Mother, I would like to see my father and brothers".

"All excuses to visit your father!"

It was only when Niru began having breathing problems that a doctor was called for the first time and that was his first and last visit.

The eldest daughter-in-law had breathed her last – the obsequies were performed with a lot of pomp and splendour. Word spread far and wide about the manner in which she was bade farewell.

Consoling Ramsunder, people described to him at length what a splendid last journey she had had.

On the other hand, a letter came from the District Magistrate, "All arrangements have been made, immediately send over my wife". Raibahadur's wife wrote back, "My dear son, I have looked out for another bride for you, hence take leave and come over immediately".

This time double the amount of money has been settled as dowry and will be paid directly.

Ek Ratri
(One Night)

Surabala and I have been schoolmates and have played the game of setting up house together. On visiting her house Surabala's mother would take the utmost care of me and murmur indistinctly to herself, "How well they are matched!"

Even at that tender age, the meaning of her words did not entirely escape me. The impression grew and became firmly ingrained in my mind that as compared to the rest of the world, I had some kind of special claim over Surabala. It was not that the heady delight of that power did not goad me into exercising that tyrannical authority. She too would patiently run all my errands and bear all the punishment meted out. The entire neighbourhood spoke highly of her beauty, but in the eyes of that barbaric youth there was no pride in that beauty. All that was sure was that Surabala had been born in her father's household merely to acknowledge my absolute over-lordship and hence was the focal point of my utter neglect.

My father was Manager to the zamindar. He greatly desired that when I was a little older, I would be initiated into the workings of the estate and put into some appropriate occupation. However, in my heart of hearts I was dead against this. Nilratan of our locality had run away to Kolkata and on completion of his studies had started work as the Collector's peon. I too nurtured such rocketing ambitions – if not the Collector's peon, without an iota of doubt, I would definitely rise to be head clerk in the courts.

I was witness to the unwavering respect with which my father regarded the legal world – the concept that every once in a whole homage would have to be paid to them by way of freshly grown garden vegetables, fresh fish and, of course, the odd few rupees here and there. So, all associated with the legal world – right down to the petty clerk were held in high esteem. They were the gods worshipped here, in Bengal – each and everyone shining constellations. Even more than the benevolent Almighty of success and achievement people depend on this genre of humanity. Hence, what the Divine had claimed in the past was rightly theirs in the present.

Following the example set by Nilratan and taking advantage of an opportune moment, I too made my way to Kolkata. Initially I put up at the house of a nodding acquaintance and later my father would financially help out every now and then. Thus the process of education continued in this manner.

Additionally, I would also participate in various organisations and committees. There was no doubt at all in my mind that all of a sudden it was imperative to sacrifice my life for the country. But, there was none to point out how this knotty goal was to be achieved or even someone who would set an example. However, that cast no barriers in the way of my enthusiasm. Ours was a rustic background; unlike the jaded palate of the urban youth, it was not our practice to jest about everything. Hence we remained resolute.

The authorities of our organisation would mete out speeches; hungry and armed with subscription books we would make our way to all the households in the fiery sunlight. Further, we would even stand with advertisements at the street crossings, organise the stage when required and rise in protest when anyone at all in any way ventured to criticise our leaders. The sophisticated urban youth would laugh and call us rustic buffoons.

I had arrived in the city with certain ideas in mind, but was rapidly moving towards something else.

At such a juncture my father and Surabala's jointly started preparations for our wedding.

I had run away to Kolkata when I was fifteen and Surabala eight; presently I was eighteen. My father was of the opinion that an appropriate age for my marriage was rapidly passing by. But it was my firm resolve to remain a bachelor and dedicate my life to the country. I told my father that till the completion of my formal education there could be no question of a marriage.

Within a couple of months the news reached me that Surabala had been married off to Ramlochan Babu, the lawyer. I was frenetically engaged in raising funds and the news appeared supremely unimportant.

The Entrance examinations were just about over when my father breathed his last. Being responsible for my mother and two sisters, I was forced to abruptly cry halt to building up my future through further studies and start looking for a job. After a lot of effort I managed to find a place as a junior teacher in a small school in Noakhali.

It seemed suitable enough for me. A lot of advice and enthusiasm would go into building up stalwart soldiers of the country. I began work, but it seemed to me that, more than the future of India, it was preparation for the impending examination that took up greater time. Any conversation other than grammar or algebra displeased the headmaster. A couple of months saw the end of my zeal.

Like a great many people bereft of talent, dreaming away their time at home, finally are pushed into the arena of work and are somehow goaded into making a living – prodded, pushed and bullied all the while. No longer is there any enthusiasm, at the end of the day it suffices to chew cud and wallow in a peaceful stupor.

For fear of an inferno a teacher stayed in the school-premises itself – being alone, I was vested with that responsibility. I stayed in a large room close to the main building.

The school was situated in a somewhat isolated ground, beside a large water reservoir. There was towering trees all around – two gigantic Neem trees cast their shadow alongside.

All this while there is a matter I have not alluded to, not deeming it necessary. Our school building was situated only a short distance away from the lawyer Ramlochan Roy. I was well aware of the fact that he and his wife – my childhood friend Surabala, were living there.

I came to know Ramlochan Babu. It remained unknown to me whether or not Ramlochan Babu was aware of my childhood friendship with his wife and it did not appear seemly to bring up such facts anew. Neither did it properly register in my mind that Surabala had at any point of time been a part of my life.

One morning during some holiday, I had dropped by Ramlochan Babu's house. I do not recollect what we had talked about – probably the pitiable conditions of modern-day India. It was certainly not that he was particularly concerned about the matter or that he was intimately associated in any manner. However, the subject matter was such that one could easily while away an hour and a half discussing such matters.

All of a sudden the muted tinkling of bangles, and wisp of a sari and gentle footsteps made it clear to me that a pair of eyes brimming with curiosity were peering at me.

In a flash a pair of eyes seared my memory – overflowing with implicit trust, innocence, and a beautiful dark pair of eyes – calm and tranquil. An iron fist unexpectedly seemed to clasp my heart firmly and a bolt of pain seared me right through.

I returned home, but the agony did not abate. In the midst of whatever I did a heavy load overcast my complete being; a sensation of agony rippled through every nerve.

In the evening, after calming down somewhat, I tried analysing – why this turmoil? My inner self responded – then, where has your Surabala gone?

My response, it is my deliberate and conscious decision to set her free. Why would she wait for me forever?

Some inner self answered. The time to make demands on her whenever you wanted is gone, no matter how desperately you might want to get even a mere glimpse of her, that is no longer possible in any way. No matter how close your childhood Surabala might be to you, no matter that you even hear the tinkling sound of her bangles, no matter that a light fragrance from her body surrounds you, what relationship might you have enjoyed?

My answer was – Let that be as it will, what relationship remains between us?

I heard the answer – Today Surabala is nobody to you, but at a point in the past, what relationship might you have shared?

That was the truth! What kind of a relationship might not we have shared? She could have been my most intimate, closest and an indispensable part of all the sorrows and joys of my world. But today she had gone so far, had become so distant – it was prohibited even to meet her, talking to her was deemed a fault, thinking of her was looked on as a sin. On the other hand, some Ramlochan – having put in a sudden appearance, by mere dint of uttering aloud a few pre-set incantations, put up an irrevocable distance between Surabala and the rest of the world.

I had no plans of setting up new norms for human society and neither did I have in mind to break down any social barriers or tear asunder any bonds. This is a mere attempt to give vent to my feelings. All the thoughts and emotions that spout forth, are they all deemed worthy of judgement. It was impossible to rid myself of the conviction that I had more right over the Surabala who presided over Ramlochan's household than Ramlochan himself. Admittedly such thoughts are illogical and unjustifiable, but entirely understandable.

I could no longer concentrate on any work. In the afternoon when the students went about their studies and the stark afternoon outside stretched far and wide, a light fragrance would waft across from the Neem tree. Then I would wish... I don't really know what I wished; all that I can be sure about is that there was not the slight vestige of desire to instil in the students the rudiments of correct grammar.

After school hours it pained me to remain in solitary silence in my room; yet, if some person came by for some light conversation, it bothered and irritated me even more. In the evening, listening to the desultory murmur of the trees all around, I would ponder — human life was nothing but a sprawling, complex web. None remember to do the right thing at the right time, and later are in turmoil — thirsting after the inappropriate at the wrong juncture.

A man like you could have been more than happy to have grown old as Surabala's husband; you desired to be a Garibaldi and ultimately turned out to be the junior teacher in a primary school. The lawyer Ramlochan had no particular urgency to be Surabala's husband, even till the last moment, marriage to Surabala was the same as marriage to any woman. However, he happily married her, continued earning; he would chide Surabala when unhappy and happily order gold ornaments when in a good mood. More or less the man leads a contented life and did not waste time brooding beside the waterside.

Ramlochan was not present for quite a number of days, having been called away on an important case. Just as I was lonely in my school room, undoubtedly Surabala too was just as solitary in her home.

I remember it was a Monday. It remained overcast from the morning and from about ten in the morning it started pouring with rain. The headmaster declared a Rainy Day holiday. Right through the day dark gloomy clouds permeated and wandered about the entire sky. The next day there was a torrential downpour, accompanied by thunder and lightning. The intensity of the storm grew as the night grew deeper. At first the gusts of winds came in from the east and then gradually from the north and north-east.

On such a night it was senseless attempting to sleep. It occurred to me — on such a night Surabala must be contending with the storm all alone. Our school building was much more sturdy than their house. It occurred to me many a time to give her shelter in my room and spend the night by the water reservoir. However, it was impossible to come to any firm decision.

When it was around 1.30 at night suddenly the air was rent with shouts – the sea is approaching... I emerged outside and went in the direction of Surabala's house. Our pond-side came before, but even at that point water came up to my knees. When I reached the bank, there was another wave.

A point of our pond-side rose to a height of almost ten-eleven feet. When I managed to clamber on top, another man on the opposite side had also scrambled up. My entire being, my very soul was in no doubt about who the 'man' was. I was just as sure that I too had been recognised.

Everything all around remained inundated in water; we remained the only two beings on an isolated island.

It was a time of turbulence and chaos, no stars in the sky cast any light and all the lamps in the world had been extinguished – at such a juncture there could be no fault in speaking even a word, but it was impossible to speak even a syllable. None even enquired after the other's wellbeing.

Both of us just remained gazing silently into the darkness. Immediately below, the dark torrential under- current of death roared by in a frenzy of madness.

Today, Surabala had cast aside the entire world and had come to stand by me. Today, there was none but me for Surabala. The Surabala of my childhood had emerged from some past birth, some mysterious enchanted evening, and in the light cast by the sun-moon and in the presence of the entire population had come and joined me. Today, after so many days, casting aside that dazzling world of light, in this terror-riddled emptiness, Surabala, all alone, had come to take her place by my side. The moment of birth had gifted me a tender unopened bud; the moment of death cast at my feet the flower in full bloom. Now, just another tidal wave, and even this distance would be broken and we would drop into nothingness, to be united forever.

That wave might not come. May Surabala live in peace and prosperity with her husband and children! Standing on the brink of this frenetic and chaotic turmoil, I savoured the taste of eternal happiness.

The night almost drew to an end – the storm died out and the waters receded – in silence and without saying a word, Surabala went back home. I too went back without uttering even a syllable.

I reflected – I was neither a clerk, nor a peon and neither Garibaldi – I was merely an unimportant junior master of a dilapidated school. In my entire life, it was only for a minute space of time that I had confronted eternity. All the nights and days of my human life dissolved and merged into that one solitary night, the true fulfilment of my worthless life.

Khokababur Pratyabartan
(The Return of Khokababu)

Chapter 1

When Raicharan first started work for the Babu, he was merely twelve. He belonged to Jessore – a scrawny lad with long hair, large eyes and a somewhat dark complexion. The boy belonged to the Kayastha clan as did his master. His main task involved looking after and lending a helping hand in all matters pertaining to the welfare of his master's one year old son.

Gradually the child grew beyond Raicharan's authority and completing his schooling and college, joined as Munseff. Raicharan was presently his personal servant.

Raicharan had another person to answer to – his master had married and brought home a bride. Hence almost all the authority that Raicharan had once wielded over Anukul Babu had practically been usurped by the new mistress.

However, just as much the new mistress had taken over Raicharan's clout, she had amply compensated by vesting him with even greater responsibility. A new child had been born to Anukul, and Raicharan – by sheer dint of his own efforts and labour – had completely taken him over.

With the greatest of enthusiasm he would vigorously swing the child. Raicharan would throw him into the air with dexterity and drawing him close shake his head in a strange manner; not waiting or expecting any kind of answer in strange tones he would sing out such questions to the child that Raicharan's mere presence would make him bubble over with joy.

When the infant started crawling and very carefully crossed the threshold and, on anyone giving chase, giggled loudly and tried to crawl at speed to a safe shelter, Raicharan would be mesmerised by his extraordinary skills and powers of judgement. He would go up to the mother and with amazed wonder reiterate, "Mother, your son will definitely grow up to be a judge and earn a lot of money."

That any other infant at a similar age could perform such a skilled task as crawling over the threshold was beyond Raicharan's comprehension. It was only future judges who had the inherent ability to perform such missions.

Finally the infant began to take the first shaky steps and that was an event of wondrous amazement! When he addressed his mother as *M*, his aunt as *Pichi* instead of the conventional *Pishi* and Raicharan as *Channa*, Raicharan took to collaring all and sundry and imparted to them this amazing and unexpected bit of information.

'The most amazing factor is that while he calls all others by their names I am addressed as *Channa*'. Truly, it was incomprehensible as to how the child could assess the mode of address. Definitely no mature adult would have reacted thus and perchance should they have done so, the average man in the street would have had enough doubt about his future prospects as a judge.

A short while later Raicharan had to grasp a bit of rope between his teeth and assume the role of a horse. It was not just that – he would also have to don the garb of a wrestler and enter into combat with the child and if he did not collapse in a heap in servile defeat – there would be a positive furore.

At about this time Anukul was transferred to a district along the banks of the river Padma. Anukul carried from Kolkata a push cart for his son. Raicharan would clad Nabakumar in satin clothes, put an embroidered cap on his head, gold bangles on both hands and silver anklets on the feet and twice a day take him out.

The monsoons came by. The ravenous Padma devoured the fields of crop of all the neighbouring villages. The wild flowers along the banks and the bamboo forests became submerged in water.

The continual sound of the banks crashing down and the wild roar of the waters resounded all around. The approaching foam made even more prominent the rapid movement of the river.

Towards the evening it was overcast, but there appeared to be no imminent prospect of rain. Raicharan's tiny whimsical master adamantly refused to remain at home and firmly took his seat in the cart. Slowly moving Raicharan came to stand at one edge of the fields, along the banks of the river. Not a single boat was visible on the river and neither was a single human to be seen in the fields. Through gaps in the clouds the confabulation between the setting sun and the radiance of the deserted silent sandy shore on the other bank was progressively being organised. In the midst of this silence, the child suddenly called out "Channa, Phoo".

A short distance away, in slushy land, a towering tree displayed a handful of beautiful bright yellow flowers – and that was what had attracted the attention of the child. A few days ago Raicharan, by dint of piercing some flowers with bits of wood, had fashioned a flower cart. That had so overjoyed the child that Raicharan hadn't even had to turn into a horse every now and then. From a horse he had straightaway been elevated to the position of coachman!

Channa was not at all inclined to wade through mud to pick flowers – quickly he pointed in the opposite direction and tried his hand at distracting the child by pointing out some flying birds. By talking such nonsensical rubbish, Raicharan started rapidly moving away.

However, a child who would one day be a judge was not one to be diverted by such wiles – particularly since there was not much to catch the eye anyway; and imaginary birds would not suffice to deflect attention anyway.

Raicharan said, "Then, you sit in the cart while I quickly go and fetch the flowers. Be careful – definitely do not even think of going near the water". Pulling up his loin-cloth till his knees, Raicharan moved towards the flowering tree.

The very fact that he had been forbidden to go near the water had the instant effect of drawing away the child's attention from the flowers towards the torrential flow of water. He observed how merrily the waters were leaping and frolicking along. It seemed as though a million mischievous child-rivulets evading a giant Raicharan's grasp, laughing all the while, running rapidly in the direction of some forbidden destination.

Their unholy example instigated the human infant. Slowly he clambered down from the cart and moved towards the water. Picking up a long strand of grass and imagining it to be a fishing line he started drawing in imaginary fish. The turbulent waves of water indistinctly clamoured and beckoned the child closer.

A soft splashing sound was heard – but so many such sounds were to be heard on the banks of the Padma during the rainy season. Raicharan picked a whole bunch of flowers. Smiling, he moved towards the cart to find nobody there. Desperately he gazed all around, but could not catch sight of a single soul.

In a flash Raicharan's blood ran cold. The entire universe appeared soiled, discoloured and hazy. Through a shattered heart he took a deep breath and desperately cried out – "Babu ... Khoka Babu ... my precious little one".

But no one cried out mischievously "Channa"; no childish tones were heard crying out in mischievous glee; only the waters of the Padma continued to flow along – in lilting merriment – as if in complete ignorance of all that happened – as if she had no time at all to spare for such unimportant and trivial matters.

As evening drew on, the anxious mother sent out servants all around. Holding lanterns aloft the servants found Raicharan like a gusty stormy nocturnal gust of wind wandering along the banks, crying out, "Babu – oh my Khoka Babu..." in broken tones. Finally Raicharan returned home and crashed down at his mistresses feet. No matter what he was asked, he kept reiterating, "I don't know, Ma".

Though it was clear to all that the Padma was behind the tragedy, suspicions could not entirely be diverted from a group of vagabond gypsies who had set up camp at one end of the village. As a matter of fact, it even occurred to his mistress that it could well be Raicharan who was behind the theft of the child. She sent for him and even pleaded in all humility, "You just bring back my child to me – whatever amount of money you want, I will give you". Raicharan could do nothing but strike his forehead in vain. Ultimately his mistress drove him away.

Anukul Babu had tried his best to drive away this unjustified suspicion of his wife against Raicharan; he had asked what could possibly be Raicharan's motive in committing this heinous crime. The wife answered, "Why, my little one was wearing a lot of gold".

Chapter 2

Raicharan returned to his village. All this while he had been childless and there was no great hope of his becoming a father either. But, it so happened that his wife delivering a male child at a late age, breathed her last.

Raicharan developed a bitter hatred towards this infant. It seemed to him that as if by wile the infant was trying to usurp Khoka Babu's place. He was convinced that having allowed his master's son to drown in the waters of the Padma, there could be no greater sinner than him were he to enjoy the joys of fatherhood. It was only his widowed sister's presence that allowed the little boy to remain in the world of the living.

What was amazing was that in a few days even this infant began to crawl across the threshold and display an unusual adroitness in evading all manner of rules and regulations and showing a lively curiosity. As a matter of fact, even the manner and tone of laughing and crying were similar to his master's son. Sometimes, all of a sudden, the sound of the child crying would make Raicharan's heart beat faster. It would seem to him that having lost his Raicharan, Khoka Babu was weeping somewhere.

Phelna, the discarded – that was the name Raicharan's sister had given the child. With time the child began calling his aunt *Pishi*. That familiar call suddenly convinced Raicharan that Khoka Babu had been unable to tear asunder his ties with his *Channa*. He had returned to take birth in his household.

In favour of this deduction there were a few irrefutable logical conclusions. First of all, this child was born shortly after Khoka Babu's sudden demise. Secondly, that his wife could conceive after so many years had to have a deeper inherent meaning. Thirdly, Phelna also crawled, took stumbling steps and addressed his aunt as *Pishi*. All the indications that presaged a future judge were prominent in him.

All of a sudden, his mistress' horrific suspicions came to mind – stunned, he thought to himself, 'No wonder a mother's heart recognised the one who had truly stolen her son'. Then, he deeply regretted all the neglect that the child had had to deal with all this while. Once again he drew near to the child.

From that point of time Raicharan began to bring up Phelna as though he were the scion of a wealthy household. He bought him satin clothes and an embroidered cap. Raicharan used his dead wife's jewellery to fashion them into gold ornaments for the child. He did not permit the child to play with boys of the locality; he turned himself into the boy's sole companion. Whenever any opportunity arose the children would tease him as a budding member of the nobility and even Raicharan's friends and acquaintances were amazed at his insane behaviour.

When Phelna reached a school-going age Raicharan sold all his property and assets and took the child to Kolkata. Somehow he managed to find a job and started sending his son to school. Raicharan somehow eked out a living but he ensured that his son ate well, dressed well and was well educated. He would tell himself, "Little one, just because out of love you have taken birth in my household, you will not be neglected in any manner".

Twelve years went by in this manner. The boy turned out to be good in studies, was fairly good-looking, healthy and had a slightly dark complexion. He was somewhat of a dandy and paid great attention to the latest hair-style and was used to a genteel life style. Phelna could not regard his father as father. This was because Raicharan treated him with all the affection of a father and yet served him in the manner of a servant. Besides, there was another reason too – Raicharan had hidden from all that he was the child's father. In the students' hostel where Phelna used to live, boys would enjoy a laugh at the expense of the village bumpkin Raicharan and it cannot be denied that in his father's absence Phelna too joined in. At the same time all the students loved the gentle and fatherly Raicharan. Phelna too was very fond of his father, but there was a tinge of hauteur mingled with it.

Raicharan was getting on in years and his master continually found fault with his work. Truly he was slacking a bit; neither could he focus on work much and was becoming increasingly forgetful. However, the man responsible for paying the salary refused to accept old age as any kind of excuse. The money that Raicharan had gathered by selling his assets was all but over. Phelna had recently taken to grumbling all the time about a lack of proper attire.

Chapter 3

One day all of a sudden Raicharan submitted his resignation and handing Phelna some money said, "Some urgent work has come up, I am returning to the village for a few days". Anukul Babu was the Munseff there at the time.

No second child had been born to Anukul Babu, his wife still nurtured the hurt of the untimely loss of her child.

One day he had just returned from the office and his wife was busy purchasing magic herbal roots from an ascetic in the hope of a child. All of a sudden a voice resounded – *Divine blessings be showered on you, O Mother*".

Babu asked, "Who is it?"

Raicharan respectfully touching his feet answered, "It is I, Raicharan".

Seeing the old man, Anukul felt a strange emotion overwhelm him. He positively plummeted him with a million questions about his present condition and proposed re-employing him once again.

A melancholic smile lighting up his face Raicharan answered, "I would like to pay my respectful regards to Ma Thakurun..."

Anukul took him along to the inner sanctum. Raicharan's former mistress did not greet him with any degree of warmth – not paying any heed Raicharan, joining both palms together, pleaded, "My mother, it is I who had stolen your son. It was neither the Padma, nor anyone else, it was this miserable I".

Anukul cried out, "What are you saying! Where is he then?"

"Sir, he is with me, I will bring him along tomorrow."

That day was a Sunday and hence, no office. Right from dawn husband and wife waited in eager anticipation. At exactly 10, Raicharan, accompanied by Phelna arrived at their residence.

Not bothering with any further questions or making any judgement, Anukul's wife, seating him on her lap, gazed at him with unrequited emotion and caressed whom she believed to be her long lost son. Truly, the boy was good-looking – there was no sign of poverty in either his clothes or demeanour. On his face was an extremely lovable and appealing look. Anukul suddenly felt an affection flooding his entire being.

However, holding on to an impassive expression, he asked, "Do you have any proof?"

"How can there be any acceptable proof for such a deplorable act as this? Only the Almighty is privy to the fact that I stole your son – nobody else".

Anukul decided that since his wife had emotionally become so attached immediately on seeing the child looking for proof would not be judicious at this stage. Whatever the truth, the best option was to accept it. Besides, where would Raicharan find such a young lad anyway.

In the course of conversation with the boy he learnt that the boy had been with Raicharan ever since his childhood. Though he identified Raicharan as his father, he had never seen paternal behaviour being reciprocated – there was always a servile attitude.

Anukul, forcibly pushing away all doubt from his mind said, "But Raicharan, you can never ever cross our threshold again".

Raicharan once again pleaded, "Master, in this old age, where can I go?"

The mistress said, "Let him be, blessings be showered on my little one. I forgive him".

The righteous Anukul said, "A crime such as this cannot be forgiven".

Raicharan, clinging to Anukul's feet, begged, "It was not me, it was the Almighty".

Noting that Raicharan was trying to pass on the responsibility for his crime onto the shoulders of the Omnipotent, Anukul was even further irritated and adamantly persisted, "It is not right to trust one who has betrayed the family in such a manner".

Raicharan left his master's feet, "That was not I, Master".

"Then who?"

"My fate."

However, such logic could not be a satisfactory explanation for any educated man.

Raicharan said, "I have nobody else in the world".

When Phelna grasped the fact that he was actually the Munseff's son and Raicharan had brought him up by dint of stealing him in his childhood, then internally he was somewhat angered. However, displaying every generosity he said, "Father, forgive him. Even if he is not permitted to stay here, arrange for a monthly pension for him".

Raicharan could only stare speechlessly at his son after such a comment; then, respectfully, he took his leave of all present and turning away became lost in the teeming millions of the world. At the end of the month, when Anukul sent some little amount as pension to his village house, the money was returned – no one by that name lived there.

Kankal
(The Skeleton)

The room next to the one in which we three childhood friends used to live had an entire human skeleton hanging on the wall. At night, the wind would blow and the clanking of bones would resound all over. During the day, we had to handle and deal with the skeletal frame. At that time we were tutored in epic poetry and in Orthopaedics, from a student of Campbell School. Our guardians nurtured a desire to all of a sudden turn us into experts in all the arts. How far this desire was fulfilled is redundant to impart to those familiar with us and to those who are not, it is best not to divulge any details.

Many years have gone by since then. In the meanwhile both the skeleton and the knowledge of Orthopaedics have disappeared God only knows where ...

Shortly after having moved elsewhere due to whatever reason, I had to sleep in that room. Not being in the habit, I found it somewhat difficult to sleep. Tossing and turning, and listening to the gongs of the clock of the Church, I had run through almost all the hours. Suddenly the oil lamp flickering in a corner of the room, sputtering for almost five minutes, went out totally. A couple of accidents already having taken place in our house, quite naturally the extinguished lamp forcefully brought home thoughts of death. It seemed to me that the manner in which this flickering flame at such a late hour of the night merged and disappeared into the darkness, the tremulous flame of life of petty humans similarly vanished into nothingness – sometimes during the day and sometimes at night.

Gradually my thoughts turned to the skeleton. Imagining what its life must have been like while alive, all of a sudden, I felt that some conscious substance fumbling along the walls was moving about alongside my bed, the sound of deep breathing could be clearly felt. It seemed to be in search of something it could not find and with increasing rapidity it continued to circle the room. Definitely the explanation was my heated brain's imagination, and the overheated blood resounded like footsteps. Even then, my skin prickled in fear. Forcefully, to rid myself of this unreasoning fear, I called out loudly, "Who is it?" The footsteps drew to a halt just by my bed and the response came, "It is I! I have come in search of my skeleton ... where it is now".

I thought it was illogical to be scared of my own imagination – holding on firmly to my pillow and lying flat, I answered with easy familiarity, "What a task to set for yourself at this hour of the night! So, is the skeleton all that urgently needed now?"

In the darkness, from very close to the bed, the response came, "What can you be thinking of! The very bones of my chest were there. Twenty-six years of my youth lay ensconced there – is it all that unnatural to want to take a look?"

Immediately I answered, "Indeed that is true! Carry on with your search, let me try and get some sleep".

It replied, "Then, you are alone, let me sit by you for a while. Let us catch up on all that has been happening. Thirty-five years ago I too would sit by human beings and indulge in idle conversation. These past years all that I have done is to make a whistling noise passing by the cemetery. Today, let me sit by you and talk like a human again".

It felt as though someone came and sat firmly beside my bed. Seeing no other option, I mustered up some enthusiasm and said, "That sounds good. Talk of something that is cheerful ... some incident of that ilk".

It answered, "If you really want to be amused, let me tell you the story of my life".

The Church gong struck two –

"When I was human and very young, there was a person I was mortally afraid of – my husband. The feelings were similar to a fish struggling against the line of an expert angler. It felt as though some complete stranger had snatched me away from the calm tranquillity of my world of water and there was no chance of a respite or reprieve. Within two months of marriage, I was widowed and relatives and friends mourned and wailed on my behalf. Putting together various signs and symbols, my father-in-law informed my mother-in-law that I was what was generally regarded in the scriptures as 'venomous woman'– innately poisonous. – Are you listening? How are you finding the story?"

"Fine! The story certainly begins on an amusing note."

"Then allow me to continue. Happily I returned to my father's household and, as the years passed, I grew older. People tried to hide this fact from me, but I was quite aware that there were few as beautiful as I was in the surrounding region. – What do you think?"

"Quite possible. But then, I have never seen you."

"Not seen me! But, how about my skeleton! Hey! Hey! Hey!– I jest … How do I prove to you that the yawning eye-sockets once were home to a large luminous doe-like pair of black eyes; there is no comparison at all between the light smile that once played on my red lips and the bare gaping cavern from which emerges this fearful laughter. When I even attempt to describe to you the luscious beauty that covered those withered skeletal bones or the soft fulfilment of youth, the sheer futility makes me laugh and angers me at the same time. At that time it was impossible for any doctor to believe that that body of mine could be used for the study of bones. There was one particular doctor who had described me as a beauteous flower to a certain intimate friend. The inherent meaning behind this was very simple – while everyone else in the world might be potentially earmarked and eminently suitable as a future sample for an orthopaedic doctor, it was only I who was the epitome of all beauty. Could a flower possibly shelter a skeleton?

"It was obvious to me that just as an unparalleled diamond emits dazzling lights of splendour whenever moved, so too each part of my body shone through with incomparable beauty, setting up tremors all around. Sometimes I would gaze enrapt at my two hands – they were such a pair that could gently leash an upstart man – such was the strength they wielded. Such examples of womanly beauty can easily be found in the mythological tales of ancient times.

"But that unadorned naked skeleton that remains bears to you false witness. Then I was helplessly mute. This is why, as compared to anyone else, you anger me the most. There is an urge to hold before you the intoxicating, fiery beauty of my sweet-sixteen youth, let sleep and languor vanish from your eyes, let the knowledge of bones beat a permanent retreat."

I said, "If you had a body, I would touch you and swear that not even a vestige of any such knowledge remains with me. And your haunting unforgettable beauty in the fullness of your youth is imprinted in bold brightness in the darkness of the night. There is no need for any further description".

"I had no companions. My brother had resolved not to marry. I remained solitary in the inner sanctum of the house. All alone I would while away time in the garden and think to myself – the entire universe continues to love me, all the stars gaze upon me, the breeze on some pretext or the other sighs deeply and brushes past me; the grassy hillock on which I sit, if conscious, would once again lapse into unconsciousness. All the young men in the world would in a group cluster around my feet – all this, all this would run through my imagination. For no reason at all, a kind of pain would permeate my entire being.

When Sashisekhar Babu graduated from Medical College and came here, it was he who came to be our family doctor. A number of times in the past I had caught quiet glimpses of him in secret. Dada, that is my elder brother, was a strange sort of man – it was as though he never properly looked at the world. The impression was that the world did not have enough space and so perforce he sought shelter in one quiet corner.

Practically the only friend he had was this Sashisekhar. That is probably why, of all men outside the family, Sashisekhar was the only one I saw all the time. In the evenings when I graciously took my place on the throne below the flowering trees, Sashisekhar, the embodiment of all men, would pay me homage. Are you listening? What do you feel?"

Sighing I commented, "If only I had been born as Sashisekhar!"

"Listen to the entire tale first."

"One overcast day I came down with fever. The doctor came on a house call. That was the first meeting.

"My face was turned towards the window so that the reddish hue of the dusk would lessen the pallor of my face. Immediately on entering, as the doctor looked at me, I tried to mirror his sight. In the light of that twilight, a slightly wan face on the soft pillow; untended strands of hair on my forehead and the lashes of beautiful starry eyes cast a shadow.

Gently the doctor told my brother, "I will need to check her pulse".

"From below the sheltering linen I stretched out a clammy, well-rounded pair of hands. I stole a quick glance at my hands – if only I could have worn blue glass bangles, it would have made an even greater impact. I have never before seen such hesitation and awkwardness of the doctor while examining a patient. With trembling, inept fingers he checked my pulse; the doctor took my temperature and I too was able to gauge somewhat the momentum at which his nerves worked – Don't you believe me?"

I answered, "There seems to be no reason for disbelief. No man's pulse runs at the same pace on all occasions".

"In the course of time, after illness and recovery, on a couple of occasions I observed that the evening court in which innumerable men gathered to pay court had gradually dwindled, and ultimately, came down to merely one. Ultimately the universe retained only one doctor and his solitary patient.

"In the evenings in secrecy, I would don a colourful sari and carefully dress my hair with fragrant flowers and take my seat in the garden.

"Why? Is gazing at oneself no longer satisfying? Truly, it is not.

"For the simple reason that I would no longer merely look at myself; I would sit alone, but take on the personality of two people. Metamorphosing into the doctor, I would stare fixedly at myself, be stupefied by my beauty and ... love and be loved, but from deep within a sigh would rent the evening air."

"From then on I was never alone. Whenever I walked, demurely I would gaze downward and observe the manner in which my fingers trod the ground and wonder about the impact this sight would have on the doctor. At midday, when the sun simmered outside the window, there was not a sound to be heard anywhere, in the sky sometimes an eagle or two would noisily soar far above; beyond our boundary walls, the toy-seller would call out in a tune of his making and draw attention to the toys and bangles he sold. I myself would lay out my bed with pristine white sheet; I would stretch out a bare hand, as if uncared for, and think – who observes this sight, who gently picks up my hand and gently kissing the heated palm softly retreats – now, assuming the story ends here, what would you feel?"

I responded, "Not a bad idea. True, the story is not complete; but imagining the end will take very good care of the rest of the night".

"But then the story becomes far too serious. Where does the sense of jest go? Where does the inner skeleton make its appearance, baring all the teeth?

"Now, continue to listen on. No sooner had he established some kind of footing, than the doctor set up his chamber on the ground floor of our house. Then, sometimes, jocularly, I would talk to him about medicines, poisons, in what manner a man could easily die and all of that. While talking of his own profession, the doctor would converse freely. Listening to him death became but a family member. Love and death – that was all that remained visible to me in the entire world.

"My story is almost at end – not much remains."

Gently I answered, "The night too is almost at an end".

"For some days I noticed that the doctor was absentminded and rather awkward in my presence. One day I observed that dressing quite nattily, the doctor borrowed the coach from my brother, wanting to go somewhere at night.

"It was impossible to control myself. Going up to my brother, after talking of this and that, I asked, 'Tell me, Dada, where is the doctor planning to go tonight in your coach?"

"The terse response was 'To die!'

"I persisted, No, tell me ..."

He answered even more abruptly, "To marry".

"Truly so?" I laughed noisily...'

"By and by, I came to learn that the doctor would be given twelve thousand rupees for the marriage.

"However, what was the point in insulting me by hiding this bit of information? Had I pressurised him by lamenting aloud – if you undertake such a course of action, I will die of sorrow? It was impossible to trust any man. In life I have come close to just one man and in a moment gained all knowledge.

When the doctor returned in the evening after calling on his patients, I laughed a lot and said, "So Doctor, you are to marry today?"

"Seeing me brimming over with cheer and happiness the doctor was not only embarrassed, but became extremely crestfallen."

"I asked, 'Then, is there to be no music?"

"At that he sighed a little and commented – Is marriage then such an occasion of happiness?"

"I laughed uncontrollably at this – such an absurd remark I had never heard before. I said – Absolutely, there must be lights and music."

"My brother was hounded so much about this that he ended up making arrangements for practically a festival of sorts.

"All that I did was talk about what would happen when the new bride came, what would be done on her arrival. I asked, 'Doctor, tell me, will you continue to move about checking the pulse of patients?'"

"Cackling with laughter, this much I am sure – though the hearts of humans, particularly men – cannot be read, I can swear that the doctor's smote him mightily.

"The auspicious hour was very late at night. That evening the doctor sat with my brother on the terrace having a peg or two; both were somewhat in the habit of doing so. The moon gradually rose in the sky.

"Smiling all the while, I went up to them and said, 'Doctor, you surely have not forgotten that it is time to start off.'"

"There is one point which needs to be made here. In this gap I had gone to the doctor's chamber and taking some powder slipped it into his glass – I had learnt from the doctor himself which powder was fatal.

"The doctor emptied the glass in one gulp and in somewhat mellow and melancholic tones said, 'Well then, it is time to leave.'

"The flutes began to resound. I clad myself in a gorgeous sari; I bedecked myself with all the jewellery in my possession and the parting of my hair I filled with vermilion – the sign of marriage. Below that flowering tree I laid out my bed.

It was a beautiful night, brimming with moonlight. All the languor and tiredness appeared to have been blown away by the refreshing westerly breeze. The fragrance of the flowers made redolent the air all around.

"When the notes of the flutes faded into the distance and the moonlight gradually darkened, when the trees and the world all around me progressively faded, I gazed wide eyed and smiled.

"It was my desire that when people found me, this light smile would like an intoxicant be still lingering on my lips. I had ardently wanted that at the moment of entering my eternal wedding chamber, this smile would still be visible.

"Where was that wedding apparel? Hearing a clanking sound I looked down to find three boys learning the mystery of the study of bones. The heart which used to beat in sorrow and happiness and where youth unfurled a new petal each day, the master pointed his cane and named the bone in question! And that last smile that had lingered – could you see any sign of that?"

"How did you find the story?"

"Quite cheery ..."

The first caw of a crow was heard; I asked, "Are you there?" There was no answer.

The rays of the morning flooded the room.

Kabuliwallah
(The Man from Kabul)

My five year old daughter Mini cannot stop talking – even for a second. She spent about a year after her birth learning the art of speaking. Ever since then, she does not waste any precious moment of her waking hours in silence. Her mother has many a time soundly scolded her and thus shut her up. But this is an impossibility for me. A silent Mini is something so unnatural that it becomes impossible for me to tolerate this situation for a very long time. It is for this exact reason that all conversations between us are conducted with a great deal of enthusiasm.

In the morning I was about to begin the seventeenth chapter of my novel, when Mini put in an appearance and began with, "Father, Ramdayal the guard called a crow '*Koua* – he doesn't know a thing, does he?"

Before I could enlighten her on the intricacies of the various languages of the world, she had already started on another topic, "Father, Bhola was saying the other day that because elephants spray the sky with water from their trunks, it rains. Imagine! Bhola can really talk such a lot of nonsense! He can only talk and talk all day long".

Not waiting for a moment for my response, all of a sudden she suddenly asked, "Father, how is mother related to you?"

Muttering an inane response I replied, "Mini, why not go and play with Bhola now, I have a lot of work in hand".

She then placed herself firmly at my feet on the ground and in no time at all became engrossed in a childish game of her making. At the time, in the 17th chapter of my novel, the hero and the heroine were preparing, under the shelter of the dark night, to escape from the dungeon by plunging into the waters of the river.

My room overlooks the road. All of a sudden Mini discarded her game and running up to the window started calling out vigorously, "Kabuliwallah, O Kabuliwallah!"

Clad in filthy loose clothes, a turban around his head, a massive sack on his back and holding on firmly to a couple of boxes, a tall Kabuliwallah was walking slowly by. I am not quite sure what kind of emotions he evoked in my daughter, but she frenetically began to call out to him. I thought, a nuisance carrying a load on his back would definitely be turning up in a short while – finishing the seventeenth chapter of my book would be an impossibility.

But no sooner had the Kabuliwallah smilingly turned around and started walking towards our house, Mini desperately ran inside and not a trace of her could be found. She had the unwavering conviction that if that huge sack could be investigated, undoubtedly, a few young children like her would definitely be unearthed.

The Kabuliwallah came up to me and smilingly greeted me. I thought to myself – though my protagonists were in a desperate situation, it certainly would not do to call the man and then not purchase anything from him.

Some purchases were made and then the conversation continued. Finally, just before he took his leave the man asked, "Babu, where is your daughter?"

Intending to get rid of her false apprehensions, I sent for Mini. She clung to my side and cast suspicious glances – once at the Kabuliwallah and once at the huge bag he carried. He delved into the sack and taking out dry fruits tried to hand them to her – Mini steadfastly refused to accept. Even more warily she sidled closer. The first introduction followed this pattern.

One evening, I had to leave the house on some urgent work. I observed that seated on a bench near the door my daughter was chattering away nineteen to the dozen; smilingly the Kabuliwallah was sitting at her feet and listening and even commenting in half-broken Bengali. In the five years of Mini's life, besides her father, never had she had such a patient and uncomplaining listener. I also notice that she had her lap full of cashew and raisins. I said to the Kabuliwallah, "Why did you do that? Please refrain in the future". I handed him a coin, which he accepted unhesitatingly and put in his pocket.

On returning I found that that coin was at the root of a storm of trouble.

Holding a shining round coin in her hand Mini's mother was scolding her, "Where did you get hold of this coin?"

Mini answered, "The Kabuliwallah gave it to me".

"Just because he gave it to you – did you have to accept?"

On the verge of tears Mini reiterated, "But I did not ask for it – he gave it..."

Rescuing Mini from imminent troubles, I brought her away.

I learnt that this was far from their second meeting. The Kabuliwallah had taken to visiting practically every day; by a judicious bribe of dry fruits, he had almost won over my little daughter's covetous little heart.

There were some standard jokes and jocular remarks that were exchanged between the two friends. On seeing Rehmat, my daughter would start laughing and ask, "Kabuliwallah, O Kabuliwallah, what is in that sack of yours?"

Responding in absolutely unnecessary nasal tones, Rehmat would answer, "An elephant". There was no subtlety in the joke, but it amused them both no end. Observing this simple friendship between the old man and the little child in the background of this festive season also brought me a strange kind of joy.

Another remark was quite frequently to be heard between them both, Rehmat would tell Mini "Khoki, little one – you must never go away to your in-law's house".

In an average Bengali household, girls are quite conversant with the concept of in-law's house from a very young age. However, having brought up our daughter on somewhat modern lines, she was not very familiar with the term. So, though not very sure about the nature of this request, it was totally contrary to her nature not to immediately come up with an answer. She would proceed to turn the table and ask, "Will you then go to your in-law's?"

Rehmat would shake his fist at an imaginary father-in-law and affirm, "I will beat my father-in-law".

Hearing this Mini would be highly amused at the discomfiture and the sorry plight of this unknown person named 'father-in-law'.

It was the beautiful festive season – in ancient times, the period when royalty set out to conquer. I had never left Kolkata to travel – which is probably why my mind travelled the whole world. In the little corner of my room, I was an inveterate traveller; my mind always yearned to see the sprawling vistas of the universe. The name of a foreign country evoked in me a wanderlust; similarly the sight of someone from foreign climes – I could clearly visualise in the midst of rivers, mountains and forests a small cottage... Thoughts of a joyous independent life-style created a picture with magnetic appeal.

But I was so tied to my room that even the thought of emerging outside felt as though a thunderbolt had struck me. This is why talking to the Kabuliwallah sitting at my desk quenched my thirst for travel to some extent.

Remote roads on both sides rocky, isolated, reddish hued towering mountain peaks; in their midst narrow mountain path along which slowly moved lengthy lines of camels. They were accompanied by businessmen and travellers – some on foot and some on camel-back. Some travelled armed, while others remained bare-handed. The Kabuliwallah, in deep soft tones, would narrate tales of all of these and the scenes would flash before my eyes.

Mini's mother was inherently wary by nature; the slightest sound on the roads would convince her that all the drunken louts that could

be found were making their way to our house. The nightmare that
the entire world was over-populated with dacoits, drunkards, tigers,
snakes and militant white-soldiers had never quite vanished from
her mind.

She was still not completely sanguine about Rehmat
Kabuliwallah. Repeated requests were made to me to keep an eye
on him. When, jesting, I tried to laugh away her fears, she asked me
a couple of questions consecutively, "Has nobody's child ever been
kidnapped; Does slavery not exist in Kabul; Was it entirely impossible
for a towering Kabuli to steal a small child".

I was forced to accept that, while not impossible, the matter
was unlikely. The same degree of belief or disbelief was not in
everybody – so my wife continued to nurture her doubts. But just
based on these suspicions, I could not forbid Rehmat to come to
our house for no fault of his own.

Rehmat would travel to his own country once annually. During
this period he would remain extremely busy collecting all his pending
dues. He would have to visit many houses, but in the midst of it all,
Rehmat would always find time to visit Mini. Observing them both,
it would truly seem that there was some sort of a conspiracy going
on. If sometime he couldn't come in the morning, he would surely
turn up in the evening. Seeing that gigantic Kabuliwallah clad in loose
clothes, in one corner of the dark room, was definitely a little
unnerving. But seeing Mini run up to him joyously and the jocular
friendship between two people with such a vast age difference truly
gladdened my heart.

One morning I sat in my tiny room, going through the proof
of my books. Before final departing of winter, the past couple of
days had been particularly chilly. Some sunlight penetrated the window
and lightly warmed my feet, leaving behind a very pleasant sensation.
It was getting on to be eight; almost all the warmly clad people all
around had finished their morning walk and returned.
All of a sudden a loud clamour was heard on the roads.

I looked out to find that Rehmat, firmly bound, was being
taken along by two guards and a line of curious boys were trailing

behind them. Rehmat's clothes were blood-spattered and one of the guards carried a bloody knife. Stepping out I stopped the guards and asked what the matter was.

Gleaning some information from him and some from the guards, I came to understand that a man owed Rehmat some money, having purchased some goods from him. Lying, he denied the debt and, in the ensuing controversy, Rehmat had knifed him.

Rehmat was addressing a volley of abuses towards the barefaced liar when all of a sudden Mini appeared crying out "Kabuliwallah, O Kabuliwallah".

In a flash Rehmat's face overflowed with a gentle joviality. Today, there was no sack across his back, hence the usual jocular remark could not be made. Mini took the plunge straightaway and asked, "Are you going to your in-laws?"

Rehmat laughed, "That's exactly where I am going".

When he saw that the answer did not amuse Mini he extended his hand to Mini and said, "I would have beaten my father-in-law, but what to do, my hands are tied".

Rehmat was sentenced to a few years' imprisonment for having caused grievous injuries.

I all but forgot about him. When, within the boundaries of our home, we went about our daily chores, it did not even occur to us how a man – an independent traveller – spent all these years in the close confines of prison.

Even a doting father must confess that, indeed, the light hearted Mini's behaviour was shameful. Very easily she forgot her old friend and established new bonds with the coachman. As she grew up these friends were replaced by female mates. As a matter of fact, these days she can barely be seen even in her father's study. You could say that in a way I have even stopped being friends with her.

The years rolled by and it was time for yet another festive season. My Mini's marriage had been fixed – she would be getting married within the holidays. Just as the divine Goddess left bereft her father and journeyed back to her husband, Lord Shiva, my darling who brought such joy would turn her father's home into darkness and leave to be with her husband.

It was a beautiful morning. After the rains, this fresh sunlight of the season appeared to be wrapped in the golden embrace of love. As a matter of fact, even the skeletal worn out concrete houses of the city took on an indescribable charm. Since the previous night the strains of the *shehnai* had been resounding in my house and with it the very bones of my heart cried out in anguished pain. The notes of the music mingled and merged with the impending sorrow of parting and permeated the surroundings around along with the warmth of the sunlight. It was my daughter's wedding day.

Ever since the morning there was chaos, with people milling all around. Temporary decorative structures were being put up all around and there was no dearth of noise and people crying out.

I was checking the accounts in my room, when suddenly Rehmat entered and greeting me stood aside.

At first it was impossible to recognise him – neither did he support the beard nor was there any sack on his back. He did not have the same robust appearance either. Ultimately it was his unforgettable smile that jolted my memory.

"Is that you Rehmat, when did you return?"

"They released me from jail yesterday evening".

The very mention of jail cast a jarring note. Never before had I seen a murderous criminal – seeing Rehmat at such close quarters my entire being cringed. On this auspicious day all that I wanted was that he would go away.

I told him, "There are certain celebrations in my house today and I am somewhat busy. It is better that you leave now".

Immediately he turned around; on reaching the door, hesitantly, he said, "Can I not meet the little one?"

It seemed that he still retained the picture of Mini as she had been all those years ago. Probably he nurtured the impression that

Mini would still run up to him crying out, 'Kabuliwallah, O Kabuliwallah'. None would cry halt to their pleasant banter. As a matter of fact, in honour of past memories, he even now carried with him a box of grapes and a few raisins wrapped in paper – probably borrowed from a fellow country man, he himself not having the means any longer.

I answered, "We are all busy at home today – it is not possible to meet anybody".

The remark seemed to upset him a little. For a while he gazed steadily at me and then with a quiet, 'Babu Salaam', he left.

My heart filled with a kind of pain. I thought of calling him back, when I looked up to find that he himself had returned.

Rehmat drew close and said, "These few dry fruits are for the little one, please give them to her".

As I tried to hand him some money, all of a sudden he firmly clasped my hands, "Babu, all your kindness I will never forget – please do not pay me. Just like your little one, I too have a daughter back home. She constantly remains with me and it is in memory of that that I bring these little gifts – trading was not my intention in coming here".

Saying this Rehmat drew from inside his loose garb a worn out and shabby bit of paper. With great tenderness he opened the folds and put it on the table.

There was the palm-imprint of a small child – it was not a photograph or any studio-picture; some soot had been smeared on a bit of paper and the touch of a beloved daughter had thus been captured. Clinging on to that memory of his loved child Rehmat would wander about the streets of Kolkata every year to sell dry fruits. It was as though that tender loving touch rejuvenated that towering gigantic rough and ready Kabuliwallah.

My eyes brimmed with tears. I no longer remembered that I was a noble Bengali with a lineage to be proud of; he and I were the same – both of us were fathers. The palm-print of his little daughter born and brought up in the rocky mountains were a reflection of my little Mini. Immediately I sent for Mini; there were a lot of protests from the inner sanctum, but I overrode all objections. A shy awkward Mini in all her bridal finery shyly appeared before me.

The Kabuliwallah was so taken aback that he lost the words of their former jokes. Finally he smiled and asked, "So, little one, you go to your in-laws?"

Mini now understood the meaning of the term; there was no ready response, embarrassed, she turned away. The memory of Mini's first meeting with him suddenly came to mind. A strange kind of ache filled my entire being.

As Mini left, a deep sigh rent Rehmat and he collapsed onto the ground. All of a sudden he clearly felt that his daughter too must have grown up and new ties would have to be forged with her. Never would it be possible to re-establish the same kind of relationship again. Who knows what had happened in the course of these eight years. That morning, in the soothing sunlight of a day in Kolkata, Rehmat could only visualise a mountain scene in far away Afghanistan.

Handing him some large notes I said, "Rehmat, return to your daughter; may the joy of your reunion shower all blessings on my Mini".

Having given away the money, some of the festivities had to be curtailed somewhat. The sparkling lights could not be afforded and neither was it possible to get the music band. The women in the inner sanctum expressed great resentment. But the lights of the wedding glowed even brighter on this auspicious occasion.

Chhuti
(The Holiday)

Amongst all the young lads, a new idea suddenly struck their leader Phatik Chakraborti. An enormous log lay by the river bank, waiting to be shaped into a mast. It was decided that all would lend a hand rolling it along.

Merely the thought of the sheer amazement, irritation and inconvenience to the owner was enough to get everybody's wholehearted support.

Just as all prepared to industriously set about the task, Phatik's younger sibling Makhanlal solemnly took his seat on it. The boys were somehow demoralised seeing his philosophical stance.

One of the group timorously stepped forward and gave him a light push, but that did not move him in the slightest. This untimely all knowing truth-seeker brooded in silence on the immovability of all sports.

Drawing close Phatik flaunted his prowess and firmly chided, "Look here, you'll only be beaten up – better move".

This only had the effect of making the lad wriggle a bit and once again take his place even more firmly.

In such a situation, in order to maintain the royal authority, it would have been the right thing if the disobedient younger sibling were firmly and sharply smacked on the head – but, courage failed him. However, Phatik made it appear such that had he actually wanted to, chastisement would simply have been a matter of raising his hand – but he deliberately chose not to undertake this course of action. This was because an even better idea had dawned on him, which could possibly provide a little more fun. He proposed rolling the log, with Makhan still seated on it.

Makhan assumed that this meant still greater honour. However, like all material honours, it struck neither him nor the others all around that such honour had as corollary other unforeseen dangers too.

The boys clustering around all lent a hand and with vociferous cries started pushing with all their might. No sooner had the stump of wood taken one spin when Makhan with all his gravity and pride came crashing down.

That the very outset would provide results beyond all hope made the boys jubilant with untold merriment – but Phatik was somewhat concerned. Makhan sprang up from the ground without wasting any time and leaping on Phatik began to blindly hit out. Scratching his nose and face, sobbing hysterically, he set off for home. The game came to an untimely end.

Uprooting some long stemmed grass, Phatik sat down on a half submerged boat in the water and continued chewing in silence.

At such a juncture an unknown boat came and anchored and a middle-aged man, supporting a shock of salt-and-pepper hair, stepped down. He asked the young boy "Where do the Chakrabortis live?"

The lad continued to gnaw and answered tersely, "There ..." – but the direction he indicated remained a mystery.

Once again the gentleman questioned, "Where?"

The reply came "I don't know" and Phatik went back to chewing impassively on the grass. Taking the help of other locals, the man continued his search for the Chakraborti.

Almost immediately Bagha Bagdi came up, "Phatik Dada – Ma wants to see you".

"I won't go."

Forcibly Bagha picked him up and carried him home; in futile rage Phatik could only struggle to free himself.

No sooner had she caught a glimpse of Phatik than his mother almost burst with fury, "You have beaten Makhan yet again!"

"I have not."

"You also continue to lie!"

"Definitely I have not – ask him."

On being asked, Makhan reiterated his former complaint and reaffirmed, "Yes, he has hit me".

That was absolutely the last straw! Going up to Makhan rapidly, Phatik gave him a sound slap saying, "You liar!"

Immediately taking up for Makhan their mother slapped Phatik hard; he thrust her away.

She screamed aloud, "What! You have the audacity to raise your hand on me!" At such a juncture that gentleman with the salt-and-pepper hair entered and commented, "What is happening here?"

Dumbstruck with joy Phatik's mother stuttered, "Oh my, but this is Dada! When did you come?" With all devotion she bent low to respectfully touch his feet.

This Dada had gone a long way on work and in the midst of it all Phatik's mother had had two children, been widowed – but there had been no contact with the brother. That morning, having returned after this inordinately long time, Bishwambhar Babu had called on his sister.

The next couple of days passed amidst great festivity. Finally, a couple of days before leaving Bishwambhar Babu had a few words with his sister about her sons' education, their mental development et al. Phatik's rebellious wayward nature and total inattentiveness as regards studies were described at great length in response and contrasted with Makhan's social calm and love for education.

His sister said, "Phatik has driven me half mad..."

Having heard everything, Bishwambhar Babu suggested that he return to Kolkata, taking Phatik back with him.

The widow lost no time in agreeing to this proposal.

She asked Phatik, "So, Phatik, what do you think of returning to Kolkata with your uncle?"

Phatik leaped up with joy, "Oh yes!"

Phatik's mother had no real objection in sending Phatik away because there was always a nagging worry that Makhan might be thrown into water or have his head cracked open or perhaps have to contend with some other major problem. But, Phatik's eagerness to leave upset her a little.

By constantly asking 'When do we leave ... when do we leave' Phatik all but drove his uncle crazy; sheer enthusiasm made him almost forget to sleep.

Finally, the sheer excitement of the journey stirred his generosity to such an extent that he willingly gifted Makhan his kite and all paraphernalia to be enjoyed down the generations to come.

On reaching Kolkata, first of all he was introduced to his aunt. It could in no way be said that the aunt was pleased at this unexpected addition to her family. She ran her household according to the norms she had laid out. In the midst of this if a thirteen year old uneducated rustic bumpkin was let loose, it very likely presaged a furore. Bishwambhar had grown in years, but did he display any practical sense!

Particularly, there was no greater nuisance in the world than a thirteen year old boy – neither was he visually pleasing, nor was he of any use at all. Not only did he not evoke any sense of affection, neither was his company particularly desirable. Any remark made by such a lad was being smarmy, a comment was utter cheek and anything said was sheer verbosity. Such a boy grew rapidly without a thought for the clothes he outgrew; people could only say that all this was unwarranted audacity. The softness of childhood and sweetness while speaking was a distant memory. The world could not help blaming him for this. A lot of faults of childhood can be forgiven, but during this phase, even a natural fault would loom large as being unforgivable.

It was also only too apparent to the boy that he did not really fit in anywhere; this was why he spent the better part of his time practically apologising for his existence and being ashamed of the same. However, it was at this very age that there was an excessive longing and craving for affection. At such a point in time, if any person displayed any signs of affection or friendship, such a youngster would become all but his slave. But none dared to show him any warmth, because to the world at large it would appear as unwarranted indulgence. Hence, in appearance the boy resembled a guardian-less cur.

Under such circumstances any place other than close proximity to a mother would be hellish. The surroundings completely bereft of any affection or softer emotions would be a continual thorny bed. At this age, women appear to such young boys as beings from a fairytale world; any kind of rejection or harshness assumes unbearable proportions.

What hurt Phatik the most was that his aunt regarded him as no better than an inauspicious constellation of stars. Perchance his aunt asked for any errand to be completed, brimming over with joy he would do far in excess of what was required. His aunt would put paid to such fervour by remarking, "That's enough, that's enough. Don't interfere with that any more – now, just pay attention to your own work. Why don't you study a little". Such disregard for his mental well-being would seem to Phatik as the most cruel injustice.

This kind of neglect at home – additionally, there was no place to breathe a little freely. Locked within the concrete boundaries, his mind kept reverting to his village.

That sprawling unending field where he would nosily fly kites and chase after them, the river where he would sing in loud shrill tones songs of his own composition as he wandered aimlessly along the banks, the narrow tributary where he would plunge in and swim whenever the desire took him, the freewheeling independent group – his constant companions – and, over and above all, his cruel and unfair mother – his mind continuously revolved around them.

An animal-like unreasoning love – just a blind desire to draw close, an unexpressed agony at not being able to see, like an orphan crying out at dusk for the maternal figure – such emotions would raise a continual turmoil in the heart of this ungainly, timid and wan boy.

There was no greater fool and inattentive student in the school. Any question would elicit just a blank stare. When the teacher began thrashing him, just as an overburdened mule, he would tolerate all. When it was playtime for the boys, he would stand by the window and gaze at the roof top of the houses far away. When in that scorching midday heat some children would appear on the roof top for a while, an impatient eagerness would run through his body.

One day, after making a lot of promises to himself and mustering up courage, he asked his uncle, "I want to go to my mother." The answer was "Let your school get over".

The festival season was still a long time in coming.

It so happened that Phatik lost his school-book. As it was, preparing lesson was an uphill task; now, it became a virtual impossibility. The teacher began to severely castigate and insult him everyday. Such a situation came to pass that his cousins in school were ashamed to acknowledge him as a relative. Any insult meted out to him, they would forcibly savour even more.

When matters became intolerable, like one who has committed a grievous crime, Phatik approached his aunt and said, "I have lost my book".

Signs of disapproval etched deep on her face, his aunt responded, "Well done! It is impossible for me to keep buying you books innumerable times a month".

Not saying another word Phatik came away. A sense of hurt grew in him that his mother was forcing him to waste the money of another. A sense of humiliation and poverty practically crushed him to the ground.

On returning from school that day he developed a headache and started shivering too. It was clear to him that he was coming down with fever and it was also apparent that this would cause his aunt no end of inconvenience. Phatik could sense only too well just what kind of an unnecessary and unwanted bother this would appear to his aunt. This inefficient and foolish boy felt deeply ashamed to even expect any kind of nursing or understanding from anyone other than his mother.

The next morning Phatik was nowhere to be found. No neighbour could give any kind of clue as to his whereabouts.

That night there was a torrential downpour. People were drenched in their search for the missing lad. Finally, unable to locate him anywhere, Bishwambhar Babu was forced to inform the police.

At the end of the day, in the evening, a car came and stopped in front of Bishwambhar Babu's house. It was still raining sporadically and a deep pool of water had collected out.

Two policemen cradled Phatik and brought him to Bishwambhar Babu. He was thoroughly sodden, liberally smeared with mud, eyes bloodshot red and shivering like one with ague. Bishwambhar Babu practically carried him inside like a baby.

No sooner did she catch sight of him, Phatik's aunt cried out, "Why go to take on all this unnecessary burden – just arrange to send him home".

Truly, an acute anxiety had permitted her to hardly have a mouthful through the day and she had unnecessarily picked on her children too.

Phatik sobbed aloud, "I was going home, they brought me back".

The fever began to spiral upwards – and the entire night he was in delirium. Bishwambhar Babu sent for a doctor.

Unseeingly Phatik stared at him and through feverish red eyes gazed bewildered at the ceiling and said, "Uncle, has my holiday yet not begun?"

Wiping dry his eyes, Bishwambhar Babu affectionately clasped Phatik's feverish hands and drew him close.

Phatik once again began to mutter, "Mother, please don't beat me... Truly, I am not at fault".

The next day, regaining consciousness, Phatik gazed longingly around the room for some eagerly-awaited person. Disheartened, he once again turned back to face the wall and lay in silence.

Understanding the cause of his sadness, Bishwambhar Babu bent down and softly whispered in his ear, "Phatik, I have sent for your mother".

The next day too went by. Hopelessly the doctor gave to understand that Phatik was taking a turn for the worse.

By the dim light of the lamp, Bishwambhar Babu sat by the patient and awaited the arrival of Phatik's mother.

In nasal tones Phatik began to cry out like navvies and count the fathoms of the river – repeating unknowing the scene that had been imprinted in his mind while crossing the river on the steamer on their way to Kolkata. It seemed the sick lad could just not gauge the depths into which he was plunging.

Phatik's mother stormed in and immediately set up a frenzy of tears. Somehow Bishwambhar Babu managed to bring her under control. She fell onto the bed and in loud raucous tones cried out, "Phatik, oh my darling child..."

As if perfectly normal, Phatik answered, "What!"

The mother once again called out, "Oh my Phatik, my little child ..."

Phatik listlessly and slowly turned to one side and without noticing anyone whispered quietly, "Ma, it is holiday for me at last – I am going home".

Samapti
(The Ending)

Chapter 1

After graduation Apurbakrishna was returning to his village from Kolkata.

The river was small and towards the end of the rainy season it had all but dried up. Presently, almost at the end of the month of *Shravana*, the waters lapped at the borders of the village and the bottom of the bamboo forests.

After consecutive days of torrential downpour, the sky was free of clouds and the sun shone brightly.

If I could have visualised Apurbakrishna's innermost thoughts, I would have definitely noted, there too the young man's emotional virility overflowing like the swollen monsoon rivers glistening luminously and as though lapping against the water.

The ferry anchored at the jetty. From the river banks the macadamised roof of Apurba's family – abode could be glimpsed between the trees. None in the house was aware of Apurba's advent and hence none had come to receive him. When the boatman attempted to pick up the bag, Apurba stopped him and joyfully moved in the direction of his home.

No sooner had he stepped down than he slipped – the ground was extremely slushy. His downfall resulted in immediate peals of melodious high pitched laughter from some concealed source and startled the birds in the nearby towering trees.

Greatly embarrassed, Apurba instantly controlled himself and looked around. He observed that on the banks, atop a pile of bricks, a girl, was laughing her head-of – it seemed she would collapse any moment.

Apurba recognised her as Mrinmayee, daughter of their new neighbour. They had lived far away, by the banks of the large river but erosion had forced them into moving; it was about two or three years since they had started living in this village.

A lot of unsavoury remarks could be heard about this girl's character. The men of the village regarded her with affectionate indulgence, but the housewives were constantly chary and concerned about her wayward and forward manners. Her playmates were all the village lads; girls of her own age evoked Mrinmayee only with the utmost contempt. This girl was the epitome of a disruptive marauder in a kingdom of children.

Being the adored daughter of her parents, she wielded enormous power. Mrinmayee's mother lost no opportunity to complain about her indulgent husband to her friends. If her father were in close proximity, her slightest tears would agonise him; keeping this in mind, Mrinmayee's mother also found it impossible to allow her daughter to shed tears.

Mrinmayee was dark complexioned and curly hair went down to her shoulders. Her comportment was similar to that of a young lad. A pair of large dark eyes showed not the slightest vestiges of awkwardness, diffidence or emotional imbalance. She was tall healthy and strong but, looking at her none even wondered about whether she was very young or old. If they had, there would have been rampant criticism of her parents for letting her remain unmarried for this inordinately long time. Whenever boats from a non-native zamindar anchored at the local jetty, the men-folk would cluster around from a distance and gaze with awe at all that was going on; women would, however, rapidly cover the better part of their faces in direct contrast to Mrinmayee who would rush to the spot clasping some child on her hips and with curly hair swinging wildly on her back. In a locale which had no hunters, in which there was no danger, like a fawn – Mrinmayee would gaze at the proceedings with unabashed curiosity; finally she would return to the boys in her group and regale them with vivid descriptions of the mode of behaviour and mannerisms of these novel beings.

Our Apurba, in the course of returning home for the holidays, had come across this unfettered young girl a couple of times and had even thought about her in his leisure and also when he was not free. One comes across innumerable visages through life, but there are some who leave an imprint on the mind straightaway. Beauty is not the sole reason – there is something else besides – probably transparency. In most people, the basic human nature cannot reveal itself; one who can with consummate ease bring that hidden nature to the fore is instantly noticeable amidst myriad crowds and in a flash leaves an indelible impression on the mind. On the visage of this young girl a turbulent femininity – like the unfettered wild deer – was always seen playing rampantly. That is possibly why her face remained instantly unforgettable to anyone who caught a glimpse of it even once.

No matter how sweet was Mrinmayee's lilting laughter, to the unfortunate Apurba there was certainly a degree of discomfort involved. He rapidly handed his bag to the boatman and, flushed red with embarrassment, quickly made his way home.

The arrangement was quite attractive; the banks of the river, the shadowy trees, chirping of the birds, the early morning sunlight and a youth of twenty. Of course, the mound of bricks was nothing remarkable, but even this hard and unprepossessing seat was made soft and appealing thanks to the person reigning supreme on it. Alas, that all the poetry that might have resulted from such a beauteous sight should be regarded as mockery! It could be designated as nothing but cruelty of fate.

Chapter 2

With the sound of that mocking laughter echoing from the one seated on the mound of bricks and wiping dried slush from his clothes and bag, walking beneath the shadow of the trees, Apurba reached home.

At the end of his meal, Apurba's mother broached the subject of his marriage. Already there were proposals; however, in keeping with the modern trends, Apurba had stubbornly insisted that he would not even consider marriage till his graduation. His mother having waited patiently all this while, there could be no further excuses. Apurba answered, "Let a suitable prospective bride be found and then a decision can be reached". His mother promptly replied, "Someone has been found, there need be no worries about that". Giving the matter some thought himself, Apurba responded, "I cannot commit till I have seen the girl". His mother was amazed at such wayward and whimsical reactions, but consented.

That night, after Apurba had blown out the lamp and retired for the night, surpassing all the sounds of a rainy night and beyond and overriding all the silence of the dead of night, a high pitched laughter began to repeatedly echo and resound in his ears. His conscience repeatedly smote him with the thought that his fall of the morning ought to be rectified by some means or the other. The young girl did not get to know, "I, Apurbakrishna, have imbibed a lot of education, lived a great number of years in Kolkata, just because of some misfortune I have slipped and taken a toss in the mud does not mean in any way that I am a mere rustic lout".

The next day Apurba was to go and have a look at a prospective bride, living in the same neighbourhood. He dressed with somewhat more care and a lot more nattily.

No sooner had he stepped into his to be in-laws' house than there was a furore of cordiality and warm hospitality. Finally, in due course of time, the girl was dusted and cleaned and painted and an elaborate coiffure arranged and wrapped, in a delicate sari, presented to the potential groom. She sat in a corner with head so bowed that it almost touched her knees and to give her courage an elderly maid stood escort behind her. A young brother of the girl studied at length the advent of this elaborately dressed stranger in their midst. Apurba, with sombre gravity, twirled his moustache for a while and then asked, "What do you study?" From the dressed and decorative mound of shyness there was no response. After repeated enquiries and gentle encouraging prodding by the maid, in one breath, the girl rapidly recited all her primary educational achievements to date.

All of a sudden there was a sudden pattering of footsteps outside and in a flash Mrinmayee appeared gasping for breath – with her curly hair swinging uncontrollably. Not even casting a glance at Apurbakrishna, she ran up to the bride's brother Rakhal and began tugging at him with all the force she could muster. At the time Rakhal was engrossed in his own observations and was extremely reluctant to move. The maid, and in low tones chided Mrinmayee without drawing attention to herself. Apurbakrishna mustered all his gravity and pride, and seriously remained unapproachable and began to shake the watch chain at his waist. Finally, finding it impossible to sway her companion, she gave him a resounding slap on the back; then she proceeded with a tug to open the to be bride's veil and then rushed out of the room in a whirl. The maid began to mutter and grumble under her breath.

Rakhal, highly amused at his sister's sudden unveiling began to giggle uncontrollably. He did not take any offence at all at being slapped – this kind of exchange was par habit between them. As a matter of fact, previously Mrinmayee's long tresses used to flow down to her back; it was Rakhal who one day had suddenly pounced on her from the back and started wielding the scissors rampantly. Angrily Mrinmayee snatched the scissors from him and chopped off what remained of her locks, which fell in bunches to the ground. This kind of exchange would continue between them.

The impromptu testing ground did not last much longer after this fracas. The girl – somehow managing to straighten herself – followed the maid back inside the inner sanctum. Apurba – twirling a practically nonexistent moustache – gravely attempted to walk out of the living room. Reaching the door he found that his newly polished pair of shoes was absent – and neither could they be located despite a prolonged and thorough search by all.

The household was thrown into a positive frenzy of embarrassment and all began to rain a shower of imprecations against the offender. Finally, no other option being available, somehow managing to slip his feet into a pair of loose, old and tattered slippers of the head of the household, the richly clad Apurba made his way back – treading very carefully in the mud and slippery slush all around.

Once again the lilting high pitched laughter was heard by the pond, in a remote corner of the village. It was as though from the midst of all the green foliage all around, the Goddess of the Forest – unable to restrain her amusement at Apurba's discordant attire – could not help laughing aloud.

Apurba came to an awkward halt and, as he was hesitantly peering all around, the shameless culprit appeared suddenly from the forest and, dropping the new pair of shoes, tried to immediately take to her heels. Rapidly Apurba clasped both, her hands and held her captive.

Twisting and turning wildly, Mrinmayee tried to unsuccessfully free herself. Streaks of sunlight filtering through the trees fell on her mischievous smiling face, framed by locks of curly black hair. As a curious traveller, bending low, gazes intently at a restless stream glistening in the sunlight, just as deeply and gravely Apurba fixed his eyes on a pair of eyes as bright as streaks of lightning. He slowly loosened his grasp and, as though leaving a task incomplete set free his captive. If Apurba had given her a smack or two, Mrinmayee would not have been surprised. But she could not fathom the cause of this incomparable silent punishment in the midst of this deserted path.

Just like danseuse Nature's anklets, the entire firmament resounded with her rippling laughter and, immersed in his own thoughts, Apurbakrishna, very unhurriedly, reached home.

Chapter 3

All day on some pretext or the other Apurba did not go to meet his mother. There was an invitation and he took the opportunity to eat out. It is difficult to understand the reason why an intelligent, grave and philosophical lad like Apurba had grown so restless and anxious to salvage his lost pride, introduce his innate greatness to a virtual nonentity an uneducated young girl. What difference could it make that a lively village girl thought him a mere nobody? For a few minutes even if she did make him to be a laughing stock and then forgetting his existence if she expressed a desire to play with a foolish unlettered village lad, Rakhal, what was the harm... What was the need for him to prove that he was engaged as a critic of a monthly journal and had a multitude of other virtues? However, it was an onerous task to explain to his own mind and Mr Apurbakrishna Roy BA was not prepared to acknowledge defeat to this rustic albeit lively maiden.

In the evening on meeting his mother she asked, "So Apu, how did you find the girl, you did like her, didn't you?"

Somewhat embarrassed Apurba answered, "I have seen some girls mother, and I did like one of them".

Even more surprised his mother asked again, "... and how many girls did you see?"

Ultimately, after a lot of hesitation, it came to light that Mrinmayee, their neighbour Sarat's daughter, was her son's choice. After so much education such a choice!

Initially Apurba felt a great deal of awkwardness, but at his mother's persistent objections that wore off. In a fit of stubbornness he asserted, "Except for Mrinmayee there is none other that I will marry". The more he recollected the other tense wrapped up bundle of a girl, the more distasteful seemed the very idea of marriage.

After a couple of days of mutual hurt feelings and sleepless nights and desisting from food, ultimately Apurba emerged the victor. His mother tried explaining to her own self – Mrinmayee was, after all, a child and her mother had been unable to bring her up rightly. Once she was married, she herself would be able to do the needful. Gradually she even managed to convince her own self that Mrinmayee was beautiful. But, almost immediately memories of her shorn jagged curly hair would surface and fill her with dependency. However, this too, she managed to persuade herself, could be rectified by dint of tightly braiding the hair and applying copious amounts of hair oil.

All the people of the locality found their own sobriquet for this choice of Apurba's. A lot of them were fond of the eccentric Mrinmayee, but not as a choice of an ideal daughter-in-law.

In due course Mrinmayee's father Ishan Mazumder was informed. He used to work for a faraway steamer company as a goods clerk.

News of a marriage proposal for his daughter brought tears to his eyes. It is difficult to assess how much of it reflected joy and how much sorrow.

Ishan Babu applied for leave to undertake preparations for his daughter's marriage. The sahib taking this to be a petty and unimportant cause refused to grant leave. Then, anticipating a week's leave during the festive season, he wrote home asking for the marriage to be postponed to that time. However, Apurba's mother responded, "There is an auspicious date this month and I cannot afford any further delay".

Having both his prayers rejected, with a heavy heart Ishan went back to his clerical duties.

Thereafter Mrinmayee's mother and all other ladies of the village began to incessantly drill into Mrinmayee correct deportment and all associated decorum. All her former activities were painted in such black colours that marriage to Mrinmayee appeared to be nothing short of a nightmare. The worried and panic stricken Mrinmayee felt that she had nothing better to look forward to life than that of a bondage and imprisonment.

Like a noncompliant and defiant pony, she dug in her heels and asserted, "I will not marry".

Chapter 4

However, Mrinmayee had to marry.

It was then that her education began. A night was all it took for Mrinmayee's entire world to become confined within the boundary of her mother-in-law's inner sanctum.

The correction process began. Apurba's mother remarked sternly, "Look, you are no longer a child – this kind of wayward behaviour cannot continue in our household".

Mrinmayee did not take the remark in quite the spirit it was intended. She assumed that if such behaviour were unacceptable here, it meant she would have to shift elsewhere. From the evening Mrinmayee could no longer be found. Finally, it was the traitor Rakhal who had her apprehended from her secret hideout. She had taken shelter in the broken chariot a short distance away.

The kind of humiliation Mrinmayee had to contend with from her mother-in-law and other well wishers can be well-imagined.

At night the sky became overcast with thick clouds and it began raining intermittently. In bed, Apurbakrishna moved very slowly towards Mrinmayee and whispered softly in her ears, "Mrinmayee, do you not love me?"

Vociferously came the answer, "No, I absolutely do not love you!" All her rage and desire to punish, like a sudden onslaught of lightning, came plummeting down on Apurba.

Somewhat downcast and disheartened Apurba remarked, "Why, what injury have I caused you?"

"Why did you marry me?"

A satisfactory answer to such a question was difficult. But Apurba reflected in his own mind: "No matter how, her incomprehensible heart will have to be conquered."

The next day, observing all the signs of incipient rebellion in Mrinmayee, her mother-in-law locked her in the room.

At first, like a newly caged bird, she paced about the room restlessly. Finally, finding no scope of imminent escape, she tore the bed sheet into shreds with her bare teeth and then fell to the ground weeping copiously and calling out to her father.

All of a sudden someone came and gently sat by her; affectionately he tried to smoothen the locks on her forehead. Vigorously Mrinmayee shook away his hand. Apurba bent low and spoke into her ear in a low voice, "I have secretly unlocked the door, come let us escape into the rear garden". Mrinmayee energetically shook her head, and, crying all the while, forcefully retorted, "No!" Trying to force her to look up by gripping her firmly by the chin Apurba said, "Just take a look at your visitor". Staring mesmerised at the fallen Mrinmayee, Rakhal was waiting dumbstruck at the door. Not looking up, Mrinmayee pushed away Apurba's hand. Apurba persisted, "Rakhal has come to play with you, won't you join him?" In tones overflowing with irritation the answer came "No!" Gauging the tense and uncomfortable situation Rakhal was more than happy to make his escape. Apurba continued to sit there in silence. Weeping for hours Mrinmayee fell asleep. Apurba tiptoed out of the room, locking the door from the outside.

The next day Mrinmayee received a letter from her father. The affectionate father in the letter bemoaned the fact that he had been unable to be present for his beloved daughter's wedding and profusely blessed the newly married couple.

Mrinmayee went up to her mother-in-law and said, "I want to see my father". Taken aback at this unexpected demand, the mother-in-law chided harshly, "There is not even a proper address for her father and she wants to visit him! Absurd and illogical demand..." Without any answer she walked away. Returning to her own room, Mrinmayee locked the door and like one who has lost all hope prayed desperately and repeatedly to the gods, "Oh father, please come and fetch me. There is nobody of my own here. I will not be able to survive here".

Deep at night, after her husband had fallen asleep, stealthily Mrinmayee opened the door and came out of the house.

Though the sky was clouding over once in a while, the moonlit night offered enough light to walk without any problems. Mrinmayee had absolutely no idea which path to follow in order to reach her father. What she did, however, believing firmly that if she managed to trace the path the postman followed in the course of delivering letters everyday, any and all addresses could be located. Mrinmayee began walking; the night almost drew to a close as her steps began to falter with fatigue. When there was a gradual stirring among the birds and one or two began half heartedly to chirp, Mrinmayee was still unsure of the hour; at about such a time she reached the end of the path which ended in a sprawling bazaar-like area. At such a juncture she was wondering in which direction to move when she heard the familiar noise of the postman, who rapidly reached the place. Mrinmayee lost no time in walking up to him and in weary woebegone tones pleaded, "I want to go to my father in Kushigunj, won't you please take me along with you?" He answered, "I do not even know where the place is..." He then left on the post-boat – not having any time to waste on kindness or answering further questions.

Within a very short while the place was bustling with life and the market place came to be teeming with life as all vendors and sellers started gathering. Mrinmayee made her way to the jetty and asked a boatman, "Can you take me to Kushigunj?" However, before he could reply, someone called out from the neighbouring boat, "Is that not little Minu, what are you doing here?" In effusive enthusiasm Mrinmayee cried out, "Bonomali, I have to go to Kushigunj, please take me there in your boat". Bonomali was a local boatman and only too familiar with this wilful and unruly young girl. He immediately answered, "You want to go to your father? Come along with me". Mrinmayee stepped into the boat.

The boatman set off. In a short while, it started raining torrentially. As the boat swayed wildly, Mrinmayee felt a deep sleep overwhelm her. She spread one end of her sari and like a true child of nature slept peacefully as the storm raged wildly all around.

On waking she found that she was fast asleep on her bed in her in-law's house. On seeing her awake the maid began to call out loudly;

her mother-in-law arrived and harshly began to berate her in no uncertain terms. Mrinmayee stared dumbly and did not have the power to utter even a single word. Finally when the mother-in-law made covert remarks about the way her father had brought her up, Mrinmayee rapidly made her way to the next room and locked the door.

Apurba, oblivious all sense of shame, told his mother, "What is the harm in sending her home for a few days?"

His mother chided him and severely rebuked him for finding no other bride but this boisterous and rowdy girl despite there being no dearth of highly suitable girls.

Chapter 5

It rained on and on, and stormy weather prevailed – both outside and inside the house.

The next day, waking Mrinmayee deep at night, Apurba asked, "Do you want to go to your father?"

Forcefully Mrinmayee grasped his hands and immediately answered, "I will".

Apurba then continued in a low voice, "Then, come, let us both escape together. I have organised a boat at the jetty".

In utter gratitude, Mrinmayee glanced up at her husband. Then she quickly got up and prepared to leave. To prevent his mother from worrying, Apurba left behind a letter.

It was the first time that Mrinmayee in total and utter dependence and willingness clasped her husband's hand and walked along the deserted silent roads at that hour of the night. The joyous turbulence of her heart began to echo and also course through her husband through the soft touch of her hands.

The boat set off at deep of night. Despite the turbulence all around, Mrinmayee fell asleep practically immediately. The next day – what freedom and what joy! On either side so many village markets could be espied and innumerable crop fields. So many boats plied on either side. Mrinmayee began to bombard her husband with questions on the most minute matters. What cargo did the boats carry, what was their destination, what was such and such places' name – all questions, the answers to which Apurba had never come across in any college text and what was beyond all experience he had garnered in Kolkata. Friends would be embarrassed to learn that Apurba had answered each and every question and majority of the responses did not have too many links with facts. However, none of that had any effect at all on the total and absolute satisfaction of the eager questioner.

The next evening the boat reached Kushigunj. Ishanchandra seated on a low stool in a shabby tin-shed, with a dirty lit oil glass hurricane-lantern, was looking through a leather bound large notebook. Suddenly the newly married couple entered the room. Mrinmayee called out, "Father!" In that room never had any human voice resounded in such a manner.

Tears began to flow down Ishan's eyes and he found it impossible to talk or react cohesively. His daughter and son-in-law appeared to be the crown prince and princesses of a kingdom; how to honour them in an appropriate manner was something he found impossible to comprehend.

Then there was the matter of a meal – that too was another concern. The poor menial was used to cooking a basic meal for himself, but on such an occasion of joy, what arrangements could he possibly hope to make? Mrinmayee said, "Father, today all of us will cook together". Apurba agreed to this arrangement with all enthusiasm.

The room lacked space and sustenance. But, just as a tiny spout more forcefully ejects water, from the caverns of poverty, joy gushed forth in vigorous abundance.

Three days went by in this manner; twice a day the steamer made a stoppage – so many people, so many clamours. In the evening silence abounded and the place was totally deserted – the three together would muddle their way through cooking with whatever was available. This was followed by Mrinmayee's inept and loving housekeeping and laughter and mock anger. Ultimately Apurba said that it was not seemly to remain behind any longer. Mrinmayee pleaded for a few days more, but Ishan said, "There is no need".

At the time of parting, Ishan clasped his daughter close and tearfully said, "My dear, be good and always remain the cause of peace and prosperity to your in-laws. Let none ever be able to find fault with my Minu".

Weeping Minu left with her husband. Ishan then returned to the doubly joyless confined little shabby room and spent day after day, month after month, regularly overseeing the weighing of goods.

Chapter 6

When the guilty pair returned home, Apurba's mother remained extremely grave and barely spoke a word. She did not make any overt complaint about any kind of behaviour, which perhaps could have been explained. This silent grievance, unspoken hurt, like the heaviest load, ever hung like a pall over the entire household.

When matters reached an impasse, Apurba went up to his mother and said, "College has reopened, I will have to rejoin for a course in Law".

His mother asked disinterestedly, "What will you do about your wife?"

"Let her remain here."

His mother promptly responded, "No, son! You take her with you". Generally, Apurba's mother used to address him a lot more informally.

Hurt, Apurba also responded immediately, "Fine then, that is what will be done".

Arrangements for travelling to Kolkata began. The day before their departure, Apurba entered the bedroom to find Mrinmayee weeping.

Suddenly his heart smote him. Melancholically he said, "Mrinmayee don't you feel like coming to Kolkata with me?"

"No!"

Apurba continued to question, "Don't you love me?" He got no answer to the question. A lot of time the response to this question was exceedingly simple; however, sometimes, thanks to human complexities, the answer was so complicated that it was too much to expect an answer from a girl of her ilk.

Once more Apurba queried, "Do you feel bad at leaving Rakhal behind?"

Mrinmayee answered with absolute ease, "Oh yes!"

This educated and qualified young man felt the sharp pinpricks of jealousy for the child Rakhal. He said, "I will not be able to return home for a very long time". Mrinmayee had no comments to make as regards this bit of information.

"...it might be two years or even longer."

Mrinmayee commanded, "While returning please get a three-edged Rogers knife for Rakhal".

From lying supine, Apurba sat up a little, "Then, you will remain behind here?"

"Yes, I will go to my mother and stay there."

Apurba sighed, "Fine, do that then... I will remain till you write and ask me to return. Does that please you?"

Assuming that an answer to such a question was redundant, Mrinmayee continued to sleep. But, Apurba found it impossible to do so; leaning against piled up pillows, he sat awake – brooding.

Very late at night, the moon rose and moonlight flooded the bed. Apurba gazed at Mrinmayee in that light. Staring at her unblinkingly, it suddenly seemed to him that she was a princess put to sleep by the touch of a magic silver stick. If only the golden-stick could be found, perhaps her sleeping soul could be awakened and a true wedding could take place between them. The silver-stick was laughter and the golden tears.

At dawn Apurba awoke Mrinmayee; "Mrinmayee, it is time for me to leave. Come along; let me take you to your mother's house". As she left the bed, Apurba clasped both her hands and said, "Now I have a plea. Many a time I have helped you in many ways – can I ask for a reward now?"

Somewhat bewildered Mrinmayee asked, "What?"

Apurba answered, "If you love me, give me a kiss".

Mrinmayee could not help laughing out loud at this strange request and Apurba's sombre expression. Restraining her merriment, she moved forward to kiss her husband, but drawing close she could not proceed any further; she began giggling uncontrollably. She gave up after two attempts, hiding her face and laughing all the while. In pretence discipline, Apurba grasped her ear lobe, shaking it lightly.

Apurba was rigidly fanatical about his resolve. He regarded as extremely degrading to forcibly demand his rights or exert himself with force. Like a veritable god he wanted to be worshipped and looked to a voluntary surrender – not stooping to garner anything himself.

Mrinmayee laughed no longer. Early in the morning Apurba walked along with her through the deserted road and to her mother's place. On return, he told his mother, "On thinking it over, I decided that taking my wife along with me to Kolkata will hamper my studies. So, since you do not want to keep her here, the best option is for her to stay with her mother".

A chasm of deep hurt yawned open between mother and son.

Chapter 7

On returning to her mother Mrinmayee found it virtually impossible to rediscover that sense of belonging. It appeared that the entire setup of the house had changed; time lagged and just did not seem to pass. Mrinmayee could not think of what to do, where to go, or whom to meet.

All of a sudden, Mrinmayee felt that through the entire house and in the entire village there was not another living soul – as though the sun had set at noon. What she just could not fathom was this intense desire to go to Kolkata – where had it been the previous day? She had not known that the life she hankered so intensely was left behind, her taste and viewpoints had changed diametrically. Like the leaf of a tree that has matured and severed itself from the stump, Mrinmayee, with consummate ease, discarded all that had constituted her past life.

According to hearsay, such weapons can be crafted which, when wielded, are capable of severing the limbs, yet leaving the victim unaware of the momentous catastrophe. The Almighty wielded this manner of a sharp sword. A resounding blow had been struck in the midst of Mrinmayee's childhood and youth – but she had remained unaware. Today the emotions awakened for the first time and Mrinmayee looked on bewildered pain and surprise.

Mrinmayee's old bedroom in her mother's place no longer seemed to be her own – the person who had lived there had abruptly left. Presently all the memories of her heart centred around that other house, another room, and another bed.

None saw Mrinmayee outdoors any longer and neither did her laughter echo all around. Rakhal was scared when he saw her and the thought of playing did not even occur to him.

Mrinmayee told her mother, "Please take me back to my in-laws".

On the other hand, Apurba's mother, recollecting her son's dismal and disheartened demeanour, felt a searing pain pierce her. It smote her in anger that Apurba had left his wife with her mother.

Under such circumstances, one evening Mrinmayee, one end of the sari covering her face, prostrated herself at her mother-in-law's feet. Immediately she was clasped in a close embrace –

mother- in-law and daughter-in-law thus uniting. Looking at her daughter-in- law, Apurba's mother was amazed. It was a different Mrinmayee and, generally, such a change was not possible for all ... Such a momentous change was indicative of significant will-power.

Mrinmayee's mother-in-law had decided that her faults could be rectified one at a time. But the Almighty, by dint of wielding some magic-wand appeared to have given her a new birth altogether.

Both were thus able to understand each other. Just as various branches constitute a gigantic tree, all diversity united and became one in that household.

This deep and calm all-encompassing femininity that overflowed in Mrinmayee caused her an inexplicable ache. Like the clouds that gradually gather in stormy and inclement weather, clouds of an unknown hurt began to pervade Mrinmayee's thoughts and emotions. In her heart of hearts she began to question, "Even if I could not understand myself, why could you not make the effort? Why did you not punish me? Why did you not make me behave in accordance with your will? If I the monster refused to accompany you to Kolkata, why did you not force me to come along? Why did you listen to me... why did you have to give in to my request? Why did you tolerate my disobedience?"

Mrinmayee recollected memories of when Apurba had held her captive by the side of the pond that morning and without saying a word had merely gazed at her, that pond, that path, that spot under the tree, the sunlight of that morning and the gaze laden with the deepest of emotions and all of a sudden she understand it all. Then, the kiss on that day of parting – which had moved in Apurba's direction and repeatedly returned empty incomplete; that unfulfilled desire returned to haunt her like a miasma, a mirage – leaving her unfulfilled. Her mind constantly reiterated – 'If only I had reacted thus under the circumstances... if only I had responded thus to the question put to me'.

A hurt had grown in Apurba with the thought that 'Mrinmayee has not completely understood me.' Mrinmayee continued to think... 'What could he have thought of me... what was his belief ...' The fact that Apurba was convinced she was just a lively spoiled girl child and not a woman who understood or loved him caused her searing pain all the time. All the kisses and caresses which remained unfulfilled she showered on the pillow. Days continued in this manner for a while.

Apurba had said, "I will not return till you write and ask me". Recollecting that, one day Mrinmayee locked her door and sat down to compose a letter. She took out the golden edged coloured paper that Apurba had left behind for her. Dipping her finger in the ink and without any thought for any grammar or pattern or neatness and in a mixture of small letters and big, in a pattern less medley she wrote, 'Why don't you write to me? How are you and come home'. Mrinmayee could not make out what else to write. What she really desired to communicate had been done, but it was human nature to elaborate a little more what was basically being communicated. That was apparent even to Mrinmayee; hence, she thought for a while and then came up with a few more additions: "Now you write to me and tell me how you are. Now come home. Mother is fine, Bishu and Punti are fine, our black cow has had a calf". She ended the letter with this bit of information. Putting the letter in an envelope, and liberally smearing each and every mark with love she wrote Apurba's name in big bold letters. No matter how replete the letter might be with love, the composition and neatness left much to be desired.

Mrinmayee did not realise that it was necessary to write something more than just the name. Out of shame her mother-in-law or somebody would see this display of emotion, she sent the letter to be posted through a trusted maid.

Needless to say, the letter got no reaction and Apurba did not return home.

Chapter 8

Apurba's mother noticed that though the holidays commenced, Apurba did not return home. She assumed that her son was still angry.

Mrinmayee too took it for granted that Apurba was annoyed with her and shrunk into herself with embarrassment at the thought of the letter she had written. She understood that the letter was so petty and expressed no true emotion at all that Apurba must have been even further convinced of his wife's childishness. As a result, he must be nurturing even more contemptuous feelings for her – the very thought made Mrinmayee write in agony. She repeatedly asked the maid whether or not the letter had actually been posted and was just as repeatedly given the answer that it was a long time since the deed had been done and her husband must have received it by now.

Finally one day Apurba's mother sent for Mrinmayee and said, "My dear, it is a very long time since Apurba has come home and I am thinking of going to Kolkata to meet him. Do you want to come along?" Mrinmayee nodded in agreement and thereafter rushing to her room grasped the pillow and laughing all the while showered her incipient emotions on it. A little later, turning grave, she grew a little anxious and depressed and started weeping.

Not informing Apurba, these two penitent ladies journeyed to Kolkata to beg for the gift of his tranquil happiness. There, Apurba's mother put up with her son-in-law.

That day Apurba, breaking his own resolve of waiting for a letter from Mrinmayee was himself attempting to write behind the locked doors of his room. However, nothing seemed to satisfy him. He sought earnest for such an address that would express his feelings of love and yet also be indicative of the hurt he nurtured. Not finding anything appropriate, there was a growing feeling of distrust of his own mother-tongue. At such a juncture he received a letter from his brother-in-law announcing his mother's impending visit and dinner that night. Despite an assurance, there was also a feeling of depression and immediately Apurba left for his sister's house.

On seeing his mother his involuntary question was, "Mother, is all well?" The equally prompt response was, "Yes, but since you have not been home for a long time, I have come to fetch you".

Apurba responded with the usual causes – his legal studies etc.

During the meal-time his sister asked, "Why have you not brought your wife along?"

The answer yet again was – his legal studies etc.

His brother-in-law laughed, "All those are trumped up excuses. It is sheer fright of us that is the only reason..."

This kind of jocular merriment continued, but Apurba remained gloomy and depressed – no conversation appealed to him. He kept brooding on the fact that if his mother could come to Kolkata, Mrinmayee might have made the effort to accompany her. Probably his mother had even made the effort to request her, but she must not have consented. An embarrassed awkwardness prevented him from putting any question to his mother. But everything all around seemed trivial and false to him.

By the end of the meal a gusty wind began to blow and a torrential downpour began soon after.

His sister said, "Why don't you stay over tonight?"

"No, impossible, there is a lot of pending work."

The brother-in-law commented, "What kind of work could there be at night... Even if you do not return one night, there is no one you have to answer to, what do you have to worry about?"

After a lot of persuasion and despite supreme reluctance Apurba agreed to stay on.

His sister said, "You are looking exhausted. Do not stay up any longer – now, just retire for the night".

That was just what Apurba was wanting; at least alone in the darkness he would be able to escape the endless session and questions and answers.

Entering the bedroom he found it was dark. His sister commented, "The wind must have blown out the lamp; well, shall I have it re-lit?"

"No, there is no need; I do not keep a lit lamp at night."

After his sister had left, Apurba carefully made his way towards the bed in darkness.

Just as he was about to get into bed, suddenly a pair of soft womanly arms embraced him and drenched him with tears and infinite kisses were showered on him – giving him no opportunity at all to even feel any surprise. At first Apurba was startled; then realisation dawned that the effort that had abruptly ended innumerable times in laughter in the past in tears had reached fulfilment in the present.

Kshudhita Pashan
(The Hungry Stones)

My relative and I were returning to Kolkata at the end of the Puja holidays when we met this Babu in a railway compartment. Initially his garb and mode of dressing left the impression that he was a Muslim belonging to the west of the country.

Conversation with him led us to even greater perplexity. He delved into all worldly matters in such a fashion that an impression was conveyed that the Almighty had consulted him before undertaking any task. We were completely free from any sort of concern that throughout the universe such strange and shattering incidents were taking place – the Russians had made unforeseen progress, the British nurtured so many secret motives, or the native kings were getting themselves into a first-rate tangle about various controversial issues. Our new acquaintance smiled beatifically and commented sagaciously, "There are more things in heaven and earth Horatio, than are reported in your newspapers".

It was the first time we had left the confined boundaries of our thresholds and hence were amazed at this man's mannerisms and way of talking. On the slightest of pretexts, he would sometimes discuss Science, analyse the Vedas or quote Persian couplets. Our amazement and reverence for his erudite nature rapidly escalated as we had virtually no knowledge of any of these subjects. As a matter of fact, the Theosophist relative of mine came to be firmly convinced that this co-traveller definitely had some kind of supernatural overtones – some sort of wondrous magnetism or divine powers or ethereal body or something of the kind. With devout attention he was reverently listening to the most banal remark the gentleman was making and in secret jotting them down. It seemed to me that even this extraordinary man was aware of this fact and it quite pleased him too!

The train came to a halt at the junction station and we all gathered in the waiting room in anticipation of our second train. It was almost 10.30 at night. We heard that thanks to some problem en route the train would be a very long time in coming. In the meanwhile, I had already laid out my bed on the table and was making preparations to go to sleep; at such a juncture, this extraordinary man began this tale. That night it was impossible to sleep –

Not having seen eye to eye on certain administrative issues, when I resigned from my work in Junagadh and joined the Nizam's administration in Hyderabad, noting that I was young and healthy, first of all I was appointed to ensure the proper collection of cotton tax dues in Barich.

Barich was a picturesque place. The river Shusta flowed through large forests, below deserted mountains along pebbled paths, like an adroit and skilled danseuse. Immediately on the banks of that river, atop a 150-step stone jetty, a white marble palace reigned in solitude – there was no human dwelling in the immediate vicinity. The cotton market and village in Barich were quite some distance away.

About two hundred and fifty years ago Mahmud Shah II had built the palace for his own debauched pleasures in this isolated place. Since then, rose scented water would spout forth from the fountain. In that quiet, tranquil and isolated seat of stone, dipping tender naked feet in the water, young women before their bath would, with open tresses, play on the sitar and sing melodiously.

Presently, the fountain no longer functioned, no longer could any melody be heard; the white marble no longer resounded with female footsteps. Now it is the residence – lonely and banished, companionless, massive and echoing with emptiness – of tax collectors like us. Karim Khan, the old office clerk had, however, repeatedly requested me not to take up residence there. He had said, "If you are adamant, stay there during the day, but never ever after nightfall". I laughed away the matter. The servants informed me that they would work during the day but would not be able to stay at night – smiling, I consented. This house was of such ill-repute that even thieves refused to try and break in at night.

Initially, the loneliness of this abandoned marble palace was like a constant heavy burden. As much as possible, I would slave during the day and at night – return, and fall into bed in exhausted slumber.

Within a week, the house, however, exuded a strange intoxication that held me firmly in its grip. It is difficult to describe my condition at the time and neither can I get anyone to believe what my plight was. Like some living being, the entire house began to gradually consume and devour me in a weird magnetic fascination.

Probably the process had begun at the moment of first stepping into the house – but I distinctly remember the day when I first consciously sensed the source.

The market was somewhat down at the beginning of summer; I had no work in hand. A little before sunset, I lay stretched out in an arm-chair on the dock of that river. The Shusta was drying up; on the opposite side, a large segment of the sandy bank took on a scarlet hue in the light of the setting sun. At the base of the steps leading to the bank close to me, pebbles glistened in the shallow clear waters. No breeze had been blowing that day. From the hills close by the heady fragrance of herbs made redolent the surroundings.

No sooner had the sun disappeared behind the mountains than abruptly a lengthy shadowy curtain dropped down on the day. Here, thanks to the mountain barriers, the mingling of light and darkness did not linger for a very long time. It occurred to me that going for a horse ride might be a good idea – with that in mind I was about to get up when footsteps occurred close by. I turned around to find the place empty.

Assuming that my auditory senses were acting up, I turned back when yet again innumerable footsteps were heard – as though a number of people were all running down together. A strange kind of fear blended together with indescribable joy caused a shiver to run through my entire being. Though there was no image before me, it was as if I could distinctly visualise a bevy of beautiful women joyously frolicking towards the waters of the Shusta to bathe. Though that evening – close to the silent mountains, on the banks of the river, in the deserted palace, there was not the vestige of any sound, I could distinctly hear, like the bubbling waters of the stream the lilting laughter of the beautiful maidens as they rapidly followed each other and moved away, passing by me. It was as though they did not even notice me. Just as they were not visible to me, I too remained invisible to them. The river remained as still as before, but I distinctly sensed that the waters were disturbed by feminine hands splashing and creating waves; the droplets of stirred water like glistening pearls scattered randomly in the sky.

My heart felt sudden twinges; I am not quite sure whether these were of fright or joy or curiosity. There was a keen desire to clearly see what lay before me, but there was absolutely nothing to perceive. It seemed that if only I could hear a little more keenly, their whispered conversation would be clearly audible. But, focussing sharply, only the murmur of the forest trees could be heard. It felt that the murky two and a half century old curtain was swaying right in front of my eyes, in timorous fright I gently uplifted one corner and cast a quick glance around – a plethora of people had gathered, but in the dense darkness nothing could be seen.

The still stupor suddenly broke with a sudden wild breeze – the tranquil and unmoving waters of the Shusta, like the untrammelled tresses of a danseuse, trembled uncontrollably. The entire shadowy evening vista of the forest creaked as though coming awake from a nightmare. Whether you designate it as truth or fiction, the unseen miasma of two hundred and fifty years ago that had been reflected in my presence vanished in a flash. The ethereal beauties who, brushing past me, with bodiless rapid footsteps and soundless high pitched laughter had plunged into the waters of the Shusta, did not return passing me, wringing water from their wet clothes. Just as the wind blows away any fragrance, with one waft of spring they too had vanished.

Then I was greatly perturbed. It occurred to me that, probably finding me alone the Goddess of Poetry would descend to prey on me. I, a poor tax collector, would become a victim. A proper meal would probably resolve these problems – it was an empty stomach that caused all such ailments!! Sending for my cook, I ordered him to literally cook up a rich Mughlai feast.

The next morning the entire matter appeared extremely laughable to me. Happily, like the white sahib, I donned a solar hat and, calling for a coach, set off for work. That day I was to submit the tri-monthly report and hence I was likely to be late. But no sooner did it turn evening than the house began to exert a strong pull. Who was responsible for this I do not know, but a hold-up was no longer possible. I had the impression that all were waiting in anticipation. Leaving behind the incomplete report and once again donning the solar hat, in the dusk, overcast by the shadow of trees and with the noise of the coach resounding all along, I alighted in front of that gigantic silent palace.

The room above the stairs was huge. Three rows of enormous columns upheld beautifully decorative structures which supported a massive roof. The sheer weight of silence of this room had an all pervasive overwhelming effect. Just prior to evening, the lamps had not yet been lit. I pushed open the huge door and entered the room, it felt as though my advent presaged a furore. It appeared that a gathering had suddenly broken up and through all the doors, windows and verandah umpteen bodiless beings made a desperate escape. Unable to actually see any of them, I remained standing in stunned silence. My entire body was flooded with a strange kind of romance. Fragrances lost aeons ago appeared to lightly waft by and stimulate my senses. Standing in the midst of those rows of columns I heard the sound of the water from the fountains falling on to the white stones, some unknown tune was being played on the sitar, the tinkling of jewels, the sonorous sound of gigantic copper bells being rung, the distant strains of the shehnai, the whizzing of the breeze blowing through the glass chandeliers, the lilting notes of song birds in cages on the verandah.

Unable to see anything anywhere, I remained standing in bewildered silence. My entire being flooded with a strange sensation. Fragrances long lost in the annals of time appeared to tickle my senses. Standing in the midst of that sprawling room – with no lamps, deserted and surrounded with gigantic stone pillars, I heard the sound of gushing water as the fountains spouted forth water on the white stones. What tune was playing on the sitar I could not understand, the tinkling sound of jewellery, sometimes the sonorous gongs of the huge copper bell, the strains of the shehnai coming from some far distance, the tinkling as the wind blew through the glass chandeliers, the trilling of the song birds in cages on the verandah – everything mingled to create a ghostly ambience around me.

Such an illusory pull so magnetised me that I felt this unreal, untouchable path where none could tread was the only acceptable truth of the world – everything else was a false mirage. The fact that I was so and so, the eldest son of late so and so, earning quite well as a tax collector, that I was attired as I was and went to such and such office on a hackney carriage – all this to me seemed so baseless and absurd that I burst into peals of laughter standing in the centre of that room.

It was exactly at that moment when my Muslim servant entered the room with a lit lamp. I don't know whether or not he thought I had turned insane; however, I do know that immediately I recollected my true identity and purpose of being there. It also passed through my mind that unseen fountains spouting forth rivulets of water or ethereal fingers stirring up nostalgic tunes – these were matters for all our great poets and composers to decide. It was an undoubted certainty that I was a tax collector and was paid for such and such work the company laid out for me. Then, once again, recollecting my inexplicable and strange fascination of just a few minutes ago, I laughed in amusement sitting at the camp table, reading the newspaper in the light of the kerosene lamp.

After having gone through the paper and enjoyed the sumptuous meal, in the small corner room I put out the lamp and went to sleep. Through the open window in front of me, an unnaturally bright star of the segment of darkness just above the Aravalli mountain range hemmed in by dense forests all around stared fixedly at the ignominious tax collector stretched out on the camp bed; seeped in amazement and curiosity, I cannot say when I fell asleep nor how long I slept. I awoke with a sudden start – it was not that there had been any noise in the room and neither could I see that anyone had entered surreptitiously. An unblinking star in the nocturnal sky had disappeared and the mild and fading moon was apologetically streaming in.

Though there was not a soul to be seen, I distinctly felt someone pushing me. No sooner was I awake than, without saying a word, five bejewelled fingers pointed delicately in a particular direction, indicating that I was to go thence.

Surreptitiously, I rose. Though in that hundred roomed palace of silent and sleeping resonance, there was not another living soul, I was frightened in case someone awakened. Most of the rooms were locked and barred and I had never visited those rooms before.

That night, with silent steps and carefully drawing in my breath, blindly following that invisible entity who beckoned, even today I cannot say in which direction I had moved. So many murky alleys, innumerable verandahs, a great number of grave, silent rooms and an equally prolific number of small, cloistered secret chambers were crossed – I lost count.

Though my unseen messenger-maid was not apparent, I could clearly visualise her in my mind's eye. A lady from Arabia, through her loose garb, her marble white firm hands were visible; from one end of the covering on her head a delicate diaphanous veil her face, at her waist hung a small curved knife.

I felt as if a night from 'Arabian thousand-and-one Nights' has flown in from the novel-world. As if I was passing though Baghdad's sleeping dark night full of danger – in search of my fiancée.

At long last, my messenger-lass halted in front of a dark-blue curtain and pointed down. Nothing seemed to be there – but my blood froze in fear.

Quite clearly I sensed, in traditional dress, a fierce and volatile African eunuch sat with an open sword on his lap, dozing, with legs widespread. Slowly and rhythmically, my emissary crossed and gently lifted one corner of the curtain.

I caught a small glimpse of the interior of the room – a Persian carpet lay spread in one corner. The person seated on the throne was not visible. All that I could see was the lower segment of saffron coloured pyjamas, two delicate feet in embroidered silk slippers – seated idly on a silken-seat. On one corner of the floor, in a bluish crystal container, were a variety of fruits, beside it two small cups and a glass bottle of golden liquor awaited the visitor. A mesmerising fragrance hypnotised my senses and held me in thrall.

Trembling, as soon as I had attempted to cross over the eunuch when he awoke with a start – the sword on his lap fell to the floor with a unholy loud clang.

Hearing a horrific scream, startled, I sat up and found myself sweating profusely – I was lying on the camp bed!! The rays of the morning sun had turned the moonlight into an unhealthy pallor; our itinerant insane Meher Ali, in keeping with his morning tradition walked along the empty streets shouting out "Keep away... Keep away".

This is the manner in which one night of my thousand and one Arabian Nights came to an end. But a thousand nights still remained.

There came to be an incongruous clash between my days and nights. Tired and worn out, I would set out during the day to complete my official duties, all the while cursing the empty, enchantress night; however, after evening, my work-bound existence seemed nonsensical, farcical and laughable.

In the evening I would become hopelessly entangled in a web of bewildered intoxication. I would become some marvellous personage belonging to some unstated, unrecorded period of history of hundreds of years ago – then, this westernised garb no longer suited me. My costume would consist of a red fez on my head, loose pyjamas, a colourful handkerchief and I would anoint myself not with modern perfume, but with fragrant attar. My seat would be atop a luxurious high and soft cushion; it was as if I anointed myself to meet my lover in a secret tryst.

Then, the more the darkness intensified, I cannot describe the strange happenings that used to take place. It was as though the scattered pages of an engrossing story of a sudden spring breeze would blow through the strange rooms of this huge palace. All would be visible till a certain distance and then no longer mesmerised, I too would blindly try to follow those whirling disparate whirlwinds.

In the midst of the mingling of these strange sensations and impressions, I would catch sporadic lightning sight of the heroine. She would be dressed in bright, colourful garb and with the fragrance of innumerable herbs and perfumes swirling around her.

She maddened me. For sheer love of her and because of the magnetic appeal she exuded, I would sink into the labyrinths and maze of dreams and move from room to room in her pursuit.

Sometimes in the evening, when placing two lamps at either end of the mirror, I would attire myself in royal style, for a fleeting few seconds, beside me on the mirror I would see the reflection of that young Iranian damsel. In a flash, turning around her graceful swanlike neck and giving only the slightest indication of some unspoken language, with the shadow of some unspoken sorrow in her dark doe-like eyes, she would just as rapidly disappear into the depths of the mirror. Stealing all the fragrance from the faraway mountains, a rough breeze would storm in and blow out the two lamps. Casting aside all my endeavours at toiletries, I would lie down in one corner of my boudoir – with eyes closed and a beatific sensation flowing through my whole being. In the breeze that was all around me, in all the mixed fragrances that wafted down from the Aravalli mountains, appeared to enfold within themselves countless caresses and kisses, fulfilling the inherent meaning of the surrounding darkness. A lot of voices were audible close to me, a fragrant breath would fall on my cheeks and the lightest, softest, most aromatic apparel would touch me. Seductively, step by step, with serpentine guile and hypnotic appeal, my entire being would be firmly bound; breathing deeply, my body, losing all powers of sensation, would fall into a deep slumber.

One evening I firmly resolved to go out horse riding – I do not know who attempted to forbid me, but that day I listened to none. As I brought down my western attire from the hook where they hung, a stormy gust of wind blew them away and along with the breeze a sweet laughter swirled about in the darkness, striking against the curtains – each note rising even higher and finally merging into the realm of the setting sun.

That day I no longer went out horse riding and from the next day I completely gave up wearing that ridiculous western attire.

Once again that night I sat up in bed and heard someone weeping as if her heart would break. It felt as though someone from the depths of a moist darkness beneath my bed, below the floor and the stone foundations of this immense palace wept helplessly, wailing all the while, "Do come, rescue me, and take me away – shatter the immense illusion, deep slumber, all the pathways of sleeps. Grasping me close to your breast and ride away with me on horseback – crossing forests, mountains, rivers – bring me to your bright and sunny room. Rescue me".

Who was I! How could I possibly rescue her? From this swirling mass of emotions and pall I would rescue which being of the ethereal world? When and where did you exist, O Divine Beauty? On which cool shore, under the shade of which fruit tree, in the lap of which being of the desert were you born? Which Bedouin marauder snatched you away from your forest climes, wrested you from which mother's womb and carrying you away across the desert sand sold you as a slave in some market! There, which royal servant surveying your budding youth counted out gold coins, carried you away across the seas and placing you in a gold palanquin brought you into the inner sanctum of royalty? What kind of history was there – in the midst of all the songs, merriment and laughter – the flash of a knife, the sting of poison, and covert glances. What endless wealth, what limitless imprisonment ... Two maidens standing on either side ensuring that always a cool breeze played ... Even the lordly Badshah languished beneath bejewelled an dainty feet. Just outside the door, like the veritable devil, gigantic eunuchs protected the privacy of the inner sanctum. Following that, what blood-curdling conspiracy, riddled with jealousy and floating along which carpet of wealth, what cruel death snatched you into its depths or you were lofted to what glory?

Suddenly the insane Meher Ali once more shrieked in agony, "Keep away... keep away. All is mirage... all is a false". I looked around – it was morning. The peon carried in the morning mail and the cook respectfully enquired as to what kind of meal was to be prepared.

I thought to myself that staying any longer in this house is impossible. That very day I shifted with my belongings to the office room. The clerk, old Karim Khan, merely smiled a bit. His smirk irritated me and, making no response I continued working.

As the day moved on towards the evening, I became increasingly absentminded – there was a growing sense of urgency of having to go somewhere; the task of calculating taxes seemed supremely superficial. The present ambience, whatever was going on all around me – everything seemed to me barren, meaningless and redundant.

Throwing aside the quill, slamming shut the large tome, instantly I sent for the coach. As if involuntarily, the coach came to a halt outside the palace just as the sun was setting at the moment of dusk. Rapidly I climbed the stairs and entered the haunted rooms.

It was silent all around. I felt as though the rooms were hushed in sullen anger. My heart swayed in violent regret – but to whom I could communicate these feelings... there was nobody to whom I could apologise. Aimlessly I began to shuffle around the silent, vast empty rooms. If only I had a musical instrument to serenade someone and sing aloud, "O flames of fire, the servile insect who had attempted to flee your presence is back again to singe his wings; forgive him this once and in the fires of your passion scorch him, burn him to ashes".

Suddenly two tear drops fell on my cheeks. Dark ominous clouds had gathered atop the Aravalli mountains. The dense forests and the smooth waters of the Shusta awaited in terrifying anticipation. The waters, the earth and the firmament all of a sudden trembled violently and suddenly a storm replete with lightning, breaking all shackles and screaming aloud in agony, raced forward rapidly. All the doors of the massive empty rooms of the palace thrashed wildly and in intense anguish wept fervidly.

That night all the servants were in the office room, there was nobody here to light the lamps. In that overcast new moon night, in the impenetrable darkness of the rooms there was the distinct sensation of a woman weeping copiously on a bed, clutching on to her untrammelled tresses, her fair visage bleeding profusely; sometimes peals of hysteric laughter rang out and at other times she wept unrestrainedly. Tearing to shreds the covering of her breasts, she beat on them, through the open window the wind thundered in and the torrential rain thoroughly drenched her.

The entire night went by – with neither the storm nor the weeping showing any signs of desisting. In futile and frenetic regret, I paced about the rooms uselessly all night. There was none to console. Who was crying aloud in such agony? What was the source of this agonised regret... What could be the source of this untrammelled upheaval?

The insane one cried out – "Keep away... keep away... all is false... all is false".

I noticed that dawn had broken and despite the stormy weather Meher Ali was walking round the palace grounds, shrieking aloud his usual warning. Suddenly it occurred to me – perhaps like me Meher Ali had once lived in the palace. Presently, despite his madness, the magnetic appeal of this stone demon drew him close into walking round the palace premises every morning.

Immediately I rushed into the pouring rain and running up to him asked, "Meher Ali, what is it that is false?"

Not paying any heed to me and pushing me aside, like the bird mesmerised in the convoluted coils of a serpent, he began to circle about the house. Desperately to warn himself, he continued to shout aloud, "Keep away, keep away, all is false, all is false..."

Despite the raging storm and inclement weather I immediately went to my office and asked Karim Khan, "Tell me, what is the mystery behind all this".

In short, what the old man said was that at one time that palace was witness to innumerable unfulfilled desires and intemperate passionate coupling – all that physical desire, the curse of the unfulfilled ardour greatly reviled each and every stone of this edifice. As a result the mere sight of a living human incited that very ardour to entrap him in coils of the hungry stones. Of all those who lived inside, only Meher Ali had emerged alive – none other managed to escape and continue to live.

I asked, "Is there any hope of escape for me?"

"There is only one option – but it is very arduous. I will tell you all – but, before that, it is necessary for you to know the history behind an unfortunate Iranian slave girl of that palace. There is no greater heart rending story."

At this juncture, the porters informed us that our train was about to draw into the station. So soon? By the time we rushed and got ready, the train arrived. From the first class compartment an Englishman was peering out and trying to make out the name of the station. No sooner did he catch sight of our friend than he ardently cried out 'Hello!' and rapidly pulled him in. We boarded a second class compartment. It was impossible to identify our friend and neither did we come to hear the end of the tale.

I said, "Finding us gullible, the man took us for a good long ride; the story is fiction right through".

Centring around this controversy, an irreparable yawning gap has been forged between my Theosophist relative and me!

Monihara
(Loss of Bejewelled Glory)

My boat was anchored at that dilapidated and weather-beaten landing jetty. The sun had set.

On the roof, the boatman was praying, mutely offering the namaaz. In the fiery background of the west his silent prayer was depicted in picturesque beauty every moment. Indescribable, uncountable resplendent colours changed – from a dark shade to light, golden to steel, from one hue to another – and were gradually fading on the surface of the still unmarked river.

I was sitting in solitude on the jetty – riddled with roots of towering trees and facing a decrepit, ramshackle mansion with half-broken windows; the chirping of the crickets sounded a melancholy tune in the silence. My dry eyes were on the verge of tears, when all of a sudden a shudder ran through my entire body as I heard, "From where have you come, sir?"

I observed an emaciated gentleman, who appeared to have been rather neglected by Lakshmi, the Goddess of Good Fortune. Just as the better part of all foreign employees in Bengal sported a time ravaged facade, devoid of all culture, he too was the same. Atop his loin cloth, he was clad in a shabby outfit, which could lead one to believe that he had just returned from work. It also appeared that at a time when a light meal was in order, he was strolling along the river banks, partaking only fresh air.

The stranger took his place on the stone step beside me. I said, "I have come from Ranchi".

"What is your line of work?"

"Business."

"What business?"

"Among other things – silk yarn and wood."

"Your name?"

Pausing a little I answered, but that was not my actual name.

The gentleman's curiosity was not satisfied. He persisted, "What is your purpose in coming here?"

"A change of air."

The man was somewhat surprised, "Sir, for the past six years I have been regularly imbibing the air here along with fifteen grains of quinine – but with no result whatsoever!"

I responded, "It will have to be admitted that there is a substantial difference between the atmosphere in Ranchi and the climate here".

"Yes, no doubt of the substantial difference. Where are you putting up here?"

Sitting on the dock, I pointed to the derelict and dilapidated house opposite and answered, "There".

Probably the man suspected that I was taking up residence in this house for I had got trace of some hidden treasure therein. Instead of entering into any further argument on the matter, he, however, contented himself with describing at length the incident that had taken place in this cursed house fifteen years ago.

The man was a local schoolmaster. An unnaturally bright pair of sunken eyes glittered in his emaciated and shrivelled visage just below an all but bald head. Looking at him I recollected the Coleridge's Ancient Mariner.

On completion of his prayers, the boatman had focussed on preparations for his meal. On fading away of the last vestiges of the dusk, the deserted dark house above the bank returned to its former, gigantic silent spectral ominous form.

The schoolmaster narrated –

Almost ten years ago, when I came to this village, Phanibhusan Saha used to live in this house. He had inherited his childless uncle's sprawling assets and business.

But, influenced by the modern era, he was educated. Unhesitatingly he entered the Englishman's office with glistering boots on and spoke in impeccable flawless English. Additionally, he even sported a beard – hence there was virtually no prospect of rising to any height in the English tradesman's office. At first sight he could be categorised as an upstart modernised Bengali.

Further, even in his house there was an added nuisance. His wife had not only studied in college, but was also beautiful – so, mannerisms and traditional behaviour were no longer applicable. As a matter of fact, even for a minor illness, the assistant surgeon would be called. There was a complete change of life style – from the old-fashioned to ultramodern.

Sir, you must be a married man and hence know all about the vagaries of women. They prefer unripe acrid mangoes, unbearable hot chillies and insufferable harsh husbands!! It is not that the unfortunate man who is deprived of his wife's love is repulsive or poverty stricken – he is merely a cowed down, unassertive individual.

If you ask the reason for this, I have given the matter a lot of thought. If a person does not cultivate his natural talent and tendency, he can never be happy. Ever since the distinction arose between a man and a woman, a woman has cultivated the art of tethering a high spirited man by innumerable wiles and guile. A wife whose husband remains submissive voluntarily is to be pitied. All the powerful weapons she has inherited from her redoubtable ancestors to quell her husband remain unutilised.

A woman inveigles a man and by virtue of her own prowess is keen on forcing love from him; presenting a good face to it, if that opportunity is not permitted, then not only is the man ill-fated, but even more so is the woman.

A man belonging to this new civilisation loses his natural, god gifted barbarianism and the modern marital relationship has thus slackened. The ill-fated Phanibhusan Saha – having emerged from the shackles of modern living as a goody-goody man – could make his mark neither in business nor in marital relationship.

Phanibhusan's wife Monimalika effortlessly gained love, without any tears got gorgeous saris and, without resorting to emotional blackmail, could easily get her husband to purchase jewellery. In this manner her natural tendencies as a woman and even her love had become sluggish. She could only accept, but not give. Her docile and simple husband assumed that the best way to receive was to give. It was diametrically opposed to the truth.

The result was that Monimalika assumed that her husband was no better than a sari or jewellery producing machinery; there was no need at all to apply any lubrication to ensure smooth running.

Phanibhusan was born in Phulberey, but his work sphere was here. Due to professional demand, the better part of his time was spent in this place. He did not have a mother living in Phulberey, but there were a host of other relatives. Particularly for them, Phanibhusan had not taken home his beautiful wife. Consequently he kept his wife away from contact with others of his family and secreted her away in this palatial house, all to himself. But, the difference between rights over a wife and all other rights is that – keeping a wife isolated from all contact does not automatically ensure that she grows closer or is that much more intimate with you.

The lady was not particularly talkative, nor did she keep much company with the neighbours. On no pretext at all did she venture to the door – even for the purpose of giving alms or fulfilling religious obligations. There was never wastage at her hands; except for the love showered on her by her husband, whatever she got, she carefully preserved. What was just as amazing was that she did not permit waste of any of her mesmerising beauty. People say that even at twenty-four she had the freshness of a fourteen year old. Those who have a chunk of ice instead of a heart, those who do not know the pain and turmoil of love, probably remain well-preserved for an inordinately long time. Just like a miser, both their interior and exterior remain insulated.

Just like lush flowering bush, the Almighty saw fit to keep Monimalika bereft of fruition – she bore no child. She was given nothing which she could treasure more than all the jewels in her almirah, which like the tender spring sun could melt the frozen compartment of her heart and allow fresh stream of tenderness to overflow.

At the same time Monimalika was extremely adept at work and never employed too many people. For her it was unthinkable that someone would be paid to do work which she was capable of doing herself. There was never a thought for anyone else and neither did she love another – all she did was work and accumulate. Hence she remained unfeeling and untroubled by any emotion; unlimited health, impassive peace and growing material assets – that was the world that encompassed her all around.

For most husbands this was more than enough; why enough, it was much sought after. The presence of a wife is like the presence of one's waist, of which one is almost unaware of until there is an ache. Excessive devotion might be commendable, but not a very comfortable situation – at least that is my opinion.

Sir, is it the job for a man to accurately measure exactly how much of a wife's love has been achieved, exactly how much has fallen short! Let a wife go about her household chores and let me go about mine – isn't that what conjugal life is all about? How much remains unsaid amidst the said, how much is lacking in what is, what remains an indication in all that is clearly stated, greatness amongst the tiniest particle – all the subtleties in this emotion of love – God has not seen fit to bestow on men and neither has it been necessary to do so. Undoubtedly women sit to analyse and reflect on the slightest gesture or indication of love or otherwise in a man. They persist in hair-splitting analysis of the actual truth in a gesture and all that is a mere gesture in the truth. This is because a man's love is the strength of a woman and that forms the basic treasure of their lives. If one can accurately steer on the basis of all this, life remains peaceful. This is why the Almighty has seen fit to endow women with this instrument of love – but not men.

What the Lord has not given, men have in recent times managed to garner for themselves. Poets scoring one over the Almighty have handed to the world at large this invaluable, all-pervasive instrument without being judgemental in any way. God cannot be blamed; he had created men and women with innumerable inherent differences. However, as civilisation moved on no distinctions remain – men display womanly qualities and women reflect masculine characteristics. Hence peace and discipline disappear from households. Now, being unable to ascertain whether it is a man or woman one is actually marrying, the groom and bride both remain in trepidation.

You are irritated! I remain in solitude, banished from closeness with my wife. Despite all this, even from afar a lot of thoughts arise about the deep, underlying truths of life. All this cannot be imparted to students; I have communicated to you – do give the matter a thought.

No matter how smooth and trouble-free the situation, Phanibhusan was distressed by a kind of uneasy discomfort. The wife had no fault at all and neither did she commit any mistake, but the husband still could not say he was happy. Taking note of the yawning gap in his wife's heart he strove to fill it to the brim with jewels and, precious stones – but, that was put into the safe and the heart remained as bereft as ever. The elderly Durgamohan did not understand all these subtleties of love, neither was his quest so heart wrenching and neither did he give with so much abandon; however, he would receive love in great excess from his wife. It does not do for a business-man to be a novice and a husband needs to be a strong man – entertain no doubt at all about this.

At just this juncture the jackals started yowling loudly from behind the shelter of the neighbouring bushes. There was a brief lull in the schoolmaster's narration. In that dark meeting ground the jackals, as if seeking to amuse themselves – on hearing the school-master's analysis of domestic bliss or perhaps getting to know of the behavioural pattern of the nouveau Phanibhusan – at periodic intervals burst into raucous laughter. After their emotional excess had died down, in the doubly heightened watery silence all around, the schoolmaster, his prominent eyes glistening even more, began his tale.

Phanibhusan's sprawling and complicated business all of a sudden had to contend with major problems. It is difficult for a non-businessman like me to explain what the problem was or even the reason behind it. To sum it up, it became very difficult for him to maintain his credit in the market. If only a certain large sum of money could be derived from somewhere and – like an unexpected streak of lightning – thrust on the public at large, in a flash all those difficulties could have been overcome and his business would flourish in full swing once again.

An opportune arrangement just could not be made. If rumours started circulating that he was looking around for funds from the local moneylenders, then his business was likely to be even more adversely affected; so Phanibhusan did his best to cope from untapped sources. None was, however, willing to lend any money without an adequate back-up.

If jewellery was kept as mortgage the entire matter could be speedily and easily resolved.

Phanibhusan approached his wife – but, not with the comfortable ease that a man can usually do so. Unfortunately, he loved his wife in the manner in which the protagonist of a poetic fantasy does his lady love. It was a love in which one had to tread very carefully and speaking spontaneously was not to be considered. It was a magnetic kind of love where, like the strong pull between the sun and earth, in the midst of it all, a yawning gap ever remained in between.

Nonetheless, even in a poetic amour, when need arose the lover would have no other option than approach his sweetheart with a hand-note and bring up the subject of a mortgage. But a faltering tune and sentences breaking up merged with confused thoughts and shudders of pain. The ill-fated and unfortunate Phanibhusan could not bring himself to say, 'My dear, there is a terrible need, give me your jewellery'.

Phanibhusan did speak, but in a feeble manner. When the stony-faced Monimalika refused to answer either in the positive or negative he was dealt a harsh blow, but did not strike back. Where Phanibhusan should have taken by force, he weakly smothered even his hurt feelings. His attitude was that – where love was the only binding force, even if disaster struck, there was no question of the application of any might. If one had been able to admonish him at the time, he probably would have put forth the argument that, in the market, even if credit is unjustifiably not given to me, I do not have the right to strike at the market. If a wife in full faith and trust does not willingly hand me over her jewellery, I cannot wrest them away. Just as credit is applicable to the market and love at home – force is justified only in the battlefield. Did the Almighty fashion man only for the purpose of evading through subtle arguments and prove his large heartedness and generosity? Did man have the time to feel the workings of his heart or did it befit him in any way?

No matter, upholding his lofty principles and ideals and refusing to touch his wife's jewellery, Phanibhusan travelled to Kolkata to try and organise funds.

Generally in life – the degree to which a wife knows her husband is far greater than the degree to which she is known by her husband; however, if a husband is very subtle, his wife cannot fathom all the intricacies. Phanibhusan's wife could not gauge her husband very well. The nouveaux men remained outside the purview of the uneducated skill of a woman which was made up of ancient traditions. They were of a certain genre. They grew to be as mysterious as women. The numerous large categories that the ordinary man can be divided into – barbarians, fools, and some blind – amongst all of them, they did not exactly fit into any category.

Hence Monimalika sent for her 'minister' for consultation and advice. A distant cousin used to work as a clerk in Phanibhusan's office. He was not one who rose by dint of his own efficiency or hard work; by virtue of highlighting his connection, he was used to collecting his salary and a little additional something.

Sending for him Monimalika made him privy to all that had happened and sought his opinion on what steps to take.

The man shook his head most knowledgeably, thereby indicating grave suspicions about the current state of affairs. Intelligent people never profess an optimistic outlook. He responded, "Babu will never ever be able to gather so much money – ultimately it is your jewellery that will be at stake".

Assessing the circumstances from her impression of people, Monimalika assumed that this was the natural course of action and that is what was likely to happen. Her grave disquietude intensified. There was no child to call her own; true, she had a husband, but Monimalika hardly felt his presence in her life. Hence, the only thing that was precious in her life was, what, like her own son, was flourishing and growing every year, what was not just silver – but, truly gold as well, what encompassed her entire world – to just think of that entirety plummeting into the depths of some business – which was a bottomless pit – made her blood run cold. She asked, "Then, what can be done?"

Madhusudhan promptly answered, "Take this opportunity and go to your paternal home with all the jewellery". The scheming Madhu had already planned how a major portion or even all of the jewellery was to come into his own clutches.

Monimalika immediately agreed to this proposal.

Towards the end of the rainy season, a ferry came and anchored at this very jetty. In the thick shrouded darkness of early dusk and to the accompaniment of the croaking of the sleepless frogs,

Monimalika, well-wrapped in a thick sheet, stepped into the boat. Madhusudhan said, "Now hand me the box of jewellery". The answer came immediately, "That can follow later – now loosen the ferry".

The boat started moving rapidly in the swift current.

Through the night Monimalika had dressed in all the jewels she was carrying; from head to toe there remained no more place. She feared that if the jewels were put into a box, they might be wrested from her. But, if she wore all that she had, none could lay their hands on them without first felling her.

Not seeing any box with her Madhusudhan could not gauge that beneath the thick sheet Monimalika was carrying her most prized assets. Monimalika might not have been able to understand Phanibhusan, but there was no mistake in her assessment of Madhusudhan.

Madhusudhan left behind a letter at the office that he was going to reach the mistress to her paternal home. The old office-manager had been employed since Phanibhusan's father's time; extremely irritated he wrote a letter to his master in error-full language and spelling, yet clearly conveyed that it was unmanly to unnecessarily indulge one's wife.

Phanibhusan correctly assessed his wife's frame of mind. What hurt him mortally was the thought that despite suffering a grievous crisis in his business, he had struggled desperately to seek funds just in order to shield his wife's jewellery; but, far from appreciating his sentiments, she was suspecting his motives! She failed to recognise him even at that stage of life.

The injustice that should have made the man fume with rage merely evoked a sense of hurt in Phanibhusan. Man is regarded as fate's justice-rod with inherent fire. If injustice fails to incite man – either against himself or against others – there can be no greater shame! That a man will flare up in abrupt volcanic fury and a woman will burst into floods of tears like the monsoon clouds for no reason at all – this was what the Almighty intends, but here it was of no avail.

Addressing his guilty wife, Phanibhusan said in his heart of hearts, 'If this be your judgement, so be it – I will carry on with my duty'. Phanibhusan should have been born when the world would move forward on the basis of spiritual strength, some five or six centuries ago; instead, he had been born in the 19th century; further, he had married a woman belonging mentally to ancient times, who was known in the scriptures to cause wanton destruction. Phanibhusan did not write a line to his wife and resolved not to bring up the subject with her in any way.

After about ten days, somehow managing to gather the required sum of money and narrowly averting the financial crisis, Phanibhusan returned home. He knew that by then Monimalika would have deposited her jewels at her paternal house and returned home. Discarding the early poor and needy attitude, and pondering on how and when the successful man would show himself, the manner in which Moni would feel ashamed and a little regretful for her unnecessary actions, Phanibhusan arrived at the bedroom door.

The door was locked. Breaking open the door, Phanibhusan entered to find the room empty. In the corner of the room the iron safe gaped wide open – totally empty of all jewels. It was as though the husband's heart was suddenly stricken. He felt that life made no sense and love as well as business and trade were all futile. It was as though family life was a cage, but within the cage was no bird. Despite all effort, the bird had strayed. Then the thought sears – with what and for what am I decorating this cage bereft of everything of value? Phanibhusan with all the emotional strength in himself cast aside this empty shell.

Phanibhusan felt no eagerness at all to start enquiries about his wife, telling himself that she would return if she wanted to. The old retainer, however, came up to him and chided, 'What purpose will be achieved by merely remaining inactive? Some kind of effort must be made to locate the lady of the house'; saying which he sent people to Monimalika's father's house. News filtered back from there that neither Madhu nor Moni had shown up there!

It was then that the search began in earnest and people began combing the river banks. In the course of the search the police were informed, but not a trace was to be found of either of them.

Giving up all hope, one evening Phanibhusan entered his empty bedroom. It was when a religious festival was being celebrated and it was pouring with rain. As part of the festivities, a fair was set up and at one end of the village arrangements had been made for local theatre groups to enact plays. The muted sound of the theatre could be heard. Phanibhusan was sitting silently, with the door swinging loosely – nothing penetrated the kind of stupor he was in. The room bore the imprint of Monimalika's touch – a glass showcase carried her favourite artefacts, her clothes as though daily used, lay hanging on the rack; a lamp that Monimalika would herself carefully trim and light lay neglected – mute witness to her last moments in the room. One who left leaving everything shrouded in silence also left behind so much history, all the inanimate objects that remained bore the living mark of her presence. Come Monimalika, return and light your favourite lamp; add lustre to your room – stand in front of the mirror and once again clad yourself in the clothes lying scattered all around. None will cherish any expectations of you; just allow your presence, your eternal youth and undiminished beauty to revitalise these numerous, scattered, orphaned, inanimate objects with your life force. The silent cry of these dumb lifeless and inert objects made the home appear nothing more than a cemetery.

At a very late hour of the night both the rain and the theatre had stopped. Phanibhusan was still sitting by the window, just as he had been all this while. Outside the window, the darkness that shrouded the surrounding was so impenetrable that Phanibhusan felt as though the veritable doors of hell were yawning wide open in front so widely that one could perhaps even catch a glimpse of objects and people long lost in the mists of time. The inimical black milieu of death might even reveal the lost golden light.

All of a sudden there was an unexpected knocking at the door, accompanied by the tinkling sound of jewels. It seemed just as though footsteps were approaching from the banks of the river. At the time the waters of the river and the darkness of the night had both merged. The suddenly joyous Phanibhusan scrambled up and tried to peer into the darkness and catch a glimpse of what was happening – but, all proved in vain, nothing was visible. The more intense the effort to see, the greater the density of the all-encompassing darkness, and the world all around seemed to become even more shadowy. At the sudden advent of visitors, Nature hastily dropped the curtain on the darkness of the night.

On reaching the top of the stairs, the sound gradually started moving towards the house, coming to a halt in front of the door. Locking the door, the watchman had gone to enjoy himself at the theatre. Blows began to be showered on that barred door, as though along with jewellery, some hard object was striking the door. Phanibhusan could no longer restrain himself. Hastily climbing down the dark stairs, he reached the front door which was locked from outside. As soon as with all his might had Phanibhusan shaken the door, that noise startled him into a state of wakefulness. He realised that, sleep-walking, he had come downstairs. His entire body was covered in sweat, his hands and feet were icy cold and, like a sputtering lamp, his heart was beating rapidly and unevenly. Shaking himself free from the cobwebs of sleep, Phanibhusan saw that all noise had stopped. It was only the noise of the rain and the distant noise of the merriment that could still be heard.

Though the entire matter was a miasma or dream, for Phanibhusan the entire matter was so close to the truth and so realistic that he felt it was only by the minute distance that he had missed drawing close to his all but impossible dream. Bhairavi, the morning music, mingling with the sound of the gushing water seemed to call out to him repeatedly that it was this state of wakefulness which was a dream, it was this world itself that was untrue.

The next day too the festivities continued and the watchman took leave. Phanibhusan ordered the main gate to be kept open all night. The guard responded, "For this merry-making occasion there are hordes of people coming from all corners of the country – it doesn't seem very wise to leave the door ajar". Phanibhusan refused to listen to reason. The guard finding no other option before him, could only answer, "Then I will stay back and remain on duty all night". Phanibhusan persisted, "That won't do – you just go and enjoy yourself". The watchman remained stupefied.

The next evening Phanibhusan put out the lights of his chamber and, like the previous day, went and took his seat by the window. In the sky, there were a plethora of rainless clouds and a weird silence of expectation and waiting cloaked the surroundings. The uninterrupted croaking of the frogs and the raucous shouts of the theatre-going crowd in no way could break the silence. The only result was a rapidly spreading bizarre strangeness.

At some late hour of the night, the noise all around gradually diminished and the dimness of the night was masked by some greater darkness. It was apparent that the time was drawing near.

Like the day before, stuttering and jingling noises resounded along the mooring jetty. However, Phanibhusan did not cast a glance. He was afraid that his intense desire and troubled efforts would not allow his yearning and efforts to come to fruition... in case the force of his eagerness benumbed his senses. He exerted all the strength he possessed to control his mind, like a wooden statue he remained still and unmoving.

The resonance and reverberation of sonorous sound moved from the steps and through the open door. Footsteps climbing the spiral staircase could be heard moving in an upward direction. Phanibhusan found it impossible to control himself any longer, his heart thudded wildly like a boat tossed about in a storm and he almost stopped breathing. The steps approached gradually and came to a halt abruptly right outside the bedroom door. Only the threshold remained to be crossed.

Phanibhusan could remain still no longer. All his pent up emotions in a flash spewed forth; in a flash he moved from the threshold, crying out piteously 'Moni!' Immediately he found himself waking up with a start, hearing his emotional outburst reverberating from the windows all around. Outside the frogs continued to croak and the theatre-chores unrelentingly went on singing with tired voices.

Phanibhusan forcibly struck his own forehead.

The next day the festivities broke up and all the actors moved away. Phanibhusan ordered that in the evening none was to remain in the house but himself. The servants were convinced that their master was engaged in some kind of mysterious occult practice. Phanibhusan remained without a morsel of food all day.

In the empty shell of the house Phanibhusan took his usual seat in the evening. That day the sky was cloudless and through the fresh clear breeze the stars could be seen shining brightly. It was still some time for the new moon to rise. Thanks to the festivities being over, hardly any boats could be seen on the river. The village not having slept during the past two days of celebrations was steeped in sleep.

Phanibhusan lay stretched out on the wooden couch, gazing up at the stars. He recollected his youth, when as a lad of nineteen, in Kolkata, he would loll on some grassy bank and dreamily stare at the stars and think pensively of his in-laws' house, where his beautiful fresh and fanciful fourteen year old bride Moni was spending her days away from him. How sweet were those days of being apart — the trembling light of the stars had created a new melody in unison with the youthful beat of the heart. Now those very stars have scripted a new massage in the sky: strange are the ways of the world!

Gradually the stars vanished from the firmament; darkness descended from the sky and obscurity arose from the earth and like eyelashes coming together in sleep, both merged into an overwhelming murkiness. Phanibhusan sat calm. He nurtured an unshakeable belief that this was the day his heartfelt desire would be fulfilled. Death would reveal her secrets to her ardent disciple.

Like the past few nights, the sound gradually ascended the stairs; Phanibhusan sat determinedly still, steeped in meditation. Passing through the unguarded doorway, the reverberation moved on and finally came to a halt just outside the bedroom door.

Phanibhusan's heart started beating in restless excitement, but he refused to open his eyes. The sound crossed the threshold and entered the dark room. The sound crossed the doorframe and entered the bedroom. It went round the room and stood at the clothes rack on which the pleated sari hung, at the hollow on the wall where the kerosene lamp stood, near the three-legged stool where the dry betel-leaf remained in its container and by the almirah full of assorted objects. It then came and stood very near Phanibhusan.

It was then that Phanibhusan opened his eyes and saw that the light of the moon had entered the chamber and directly in front of his couch stood a skeleton. That skeletal being was resplendent in bejewelled glory. What was most fearful was that her eyes glistened and shone with life – they retained every vestige of calm determination and unperturbed tranquillity. Eighteen years ago, in a brightly lit hall, to the tune of the Sahana raga being played on the shehnai, Phanibhusan had first seen the beautiful, lustrous black eyes during the auspicious exchange of looks between the bride and the groom. Those very eyes, when seen at midnight, in the fading moonlight, made Phanibhusan's blood freeze. He tried his best to close his eyes, but that was an impossibility. They continued to stare unblinkingly like the eyes of a dead man.

It was at that moment that the skeleton, fixing her eyes firmly on Phanibhusan's face, and pointing her index finger, beckoned him closer. The diamond rings on the skeletal fingers glittered and shone. Like a mesmerised doll, Phanibhusan blindly followed as she walked through the house and down the stairs. Finally, both moved onto the garden-road. At last they crossed the courtyard and came upon a garden lane, paved with small brick pieces. The bones made a grating noise. The faint light of the moon that was visible through the dense branches could not find any escape. Through that rain-scented, dark, shadowy pathway, amidst the cluster of fireflies, the two found their way to the banks of the river.

Treading along the same path and to the accompaniment of a harsh sound, the skeleton moved down to the river. The turbulent monsoon river glistened, shining in the moonlight.

Along with the skeleton, Phanibhusan also stepped into the river. Contact with water had the immediate effect of shaking him awake. There was none ahead of him to show the way; the only mute witnesses were the shadowy trees on the banks of the river and overhead the moon gazed on in surprised silence. Shuddering repeatedly and unable to stop himself from slipping, Phanibhusan fell into the river. Though he did know swimming, Phanibhusan's nerves and senses were not in his control; coming awake for just a few seconds, once more he slipped into a state of infinite slumber.

Completing the story, the schoolmaster paused for a while. No sooner had he stopped, than it became only too apparent that the entire world around him had also fallen silent. For a long long while I did not speak a word and in the darkness neither could he make out my expression.

He remarked, "You did not believe my story?"

"Do you believe in it yourself?"

"No, and allow me to give you just some reasons why. First of all, Mother Nature has a lot to do – she has no time to devote to writing novels.

I added, "Secondly, my name is Phanibhusan Saha".

Not showing a whit of shame the schoolmaster went on, "Then, my guess was right! What was your wife's name?"

I answered, "Netyakali ..."

Nashtaneer
(Broken Nest)

Chapter 1

There was no need for Bhupati to earn a living. He had more than enough money and at the time the country too was in a state of turbulence. However, the stars had decided that he was to be born a man of action and so vested him with the responsibility of publishing an English journal. From then on he had absolutely no cause to grumble about lengthy periods of inactivity.

Since childhood Bhupati nurtured ambitions of writing and holding forth in English. Even without any pressing need, he would write letters to newspapers; should there be no issue to address, he would still ensure making a remark or two at any public function.

In a bid to wean a wealthy sponsor like him in their fold, various political parties would laud him to the skies with innumerable platitudes. As a result, an inflated impression of his prowess over the English language had been engendered – "The outstanding talents you have ..." etc.

Bhupati was greatly enthused. There was no pride in having one's letters published in a journal belonging to another; in a newspaper belonging solely to him, he could give full vent to all his inherent creative powers. Engaging his brother-in-law as his assistance, at a rather young age Bhupati ascended to the post of editor.

The heady intoxication of editorship and political involvement can hold one in thrall very strongly. Neither was there any dearth of people to instigate Bhupati.

In this manner, all the while that he remained enmeshed in the newspaper, his child bride Charulata had crossed the threshold and was on the brink of blossoming youth. The editor of the newspaper was unaware of this momentous event. The main target and focus was the Indian Government's border policy which was straining at the seams and threatening to break free of all bonds.

In a wealthy household, Charulata had no work at all. Just like a senseless flowering, her only task was to unfold to fruition. She had no need that remained unfulfilled.

Under such circumstances, finding an opportune moment, a young woman tends to go overboard, surpassing all limits and boundaries of married life and move towards what remains undecided. Charulata had no such opportunity. It was practically impossible for her to penetrate the armour of the newspaper and establish rights over her husband.

Some kind relatives drawing his attention towards his wife brimming with youthful beauty and chiding him, Bhupati came to awareness and said, "Well, true enough, Charu should have some kind of companion, poor girl has nothing at all to do all day".

Bhupati told his brother-in-law Umapati, "Why don't you send for your wife; there are no women of her own age group – Charu must be feeling extremely lonely all day".

The editor clearly understood that it was merely lack of female companionship that was a cause of sorrow for his wife and setting up his brother-in-law's wife Mandakini in his own household he breathed a sigh of relief.

At the first dawn of love, husband and wife draw closer to each other; when that golden moment of togetherness slipped away in oblivion none was even aware. Without having savoured the heady delight of the novelties of first love, the sweet and sour passions of youthful romance, the relationship slipped into stale familiarity.

As Charulata had a natural leaning towards studies and learning, her days had not become too burdensome. By dint of her

own efforts and taking recourse to any number of guiles she had
organised lessons for herself. Bhupati's cousin Amal was a third year
college student; Charulata would somehow get him to teach her. In
lieu, Charulata would have to put up with any number of demands
and foibles. She would frequently have to sponsor Amal's eating
forays and also pay for his passion for English literature. Further,
once in a while Amal would invite his friends over for meals and
who else but Charulata would take it on herself to ensure the smooth
functioning of all such arrangements. Bhupati, her husband, made
no demands of Charulata; but, there was no end to the endless
requirements of her brother-in-law Amal. Sometimes Charulata
would give vent to a mock anger and threaten to throw away all
such shackles. However, the advent of some person or the other
and this kind of affectionate tyranny had become absolutely essential
for her.

Amal said, "There are certain people in our college who come
wearing such eye catching shoes that it is positively intolerable – I
just have to have a similar pair of shoes, or else my pride can no
longer take such a beating".

Charu, "... and why not, of course I have nothing better to do
with my time than to knit such fashionable shoes for you. I am giving
you some money – make arrangements to get it from the market".

"No, that is definitely not the answer to my problem."

Charu not only had any idea how to fashion such shoes, but
also was determined not to expose her ignorance to Amal. She had
no option but to accede to the pleas of that unique member of the
household who makes unique demands on her. Surreptitiously – when
Amal was in college – Charu carefully learnt the art of making these
fancy slippers and by the time, Amal was beginning to forget about
this demand, one evening she invited him over.

During a summer evening arrangements had been made for
Amal's meal on the terrace upstairs. For fear of dust and sand spoiling
the food, the dishes had been kept covered. Having changed and

freshened up from his stint in college, Amal appeared looking dapper and fresh.

Comfortably seating himself, Amal opened the dish, only to find himself staring at a pair of embroidered slippers. Charulata clapped her hands and laughed aloud in glee.

His demand for shoes having been successfully met, Amal grew even more ambitious and began to frequently make any number of outrageous demands.

Charulata vociferously protested each time and just as staunchly made sure that Amal got exactly what he was looking for. Sometimes Amal would keep an eye and enquire, "Well, and how far have you progressed?"

In jest Charulata would respond, "Absolutely none!" Sometimes she would also say, "That has completely slipped my memory".

Amal was not one to let go so easily — he would persistently reiterate his demands. Deliberately instigating these unjustified demands, Charu would put up a show of opposing him and suddenly surprise him by handing him the desired object. It was in the fulfilment of these loving demands that she found fulfilment and contentment.

It would be too much to call the small patch of land that lay in Bhupati's inner sanctum a garden. A small fruit tree was the only noteworthy foliage.

Amal and Charu between them had set up a committee for the betterment of this plot of land. Both together had drawn up elaborate plans — through sketches and plans et al...

Amal remarked, "Like the princesses of the past, you yourself will have to water all the plants in the garden".

Charu said, "A little cottage will have to be put up in the western corner for our pet doe".

Amal answered, "A small reservoir will also have to be excavated and that will be the abode of ducks".

Enthusiastically greeting this suggestion Charu said, "We will plant blue lotus there; that has been my secret desire for a long long time".

Amal went on, "A small bridge can be forged across that reservoir and on its banks will be anchored a small ferry".

Charu, "Of course, the landing dock will be bound in white marble."

Amal set about making elaborate arrangements for a map.

Thanks to their combined plans and suggestions, any number of maps were drawn up in the next couple of days.

Once some sort of a map was made, an estimate was made of the cost involved. The first decision had been that Charu would contribute to gradually building up the garden from the monthly sum of money for her personal use. Bhupati remained unaware of what went about in the house; he would be summoned on completion and given a big surprise. He would definitely assume that it was the magic lamp of Aladdin that had wrought such beauty and transported it across the oceans, from Japan.

Despite lowering the costs as much as possible, however, it still proved far beyond Charu's means. Amal then once again set about changing the map and said, "Then the water reservoir will have to be done away with".

Charu immediately answered, "No, no, that is impossible, that is where my blue lotus is to flower".

Amal continued, "Does it really matter if your deer house does not have tiles? Just a plain thatched roof should do fine".

Angrily Charu retorted, "Then, I have no use for the room – let it be".

There had been plans to import spices from overseas, but no sooner had Amal proposed as a substitute the ordinary variety from local Maniktala that Charu turned quietly sullen; She only remarked, "Then, I have no use for a garden".

This was not the means to adopt in reducing costs. It was practically impossible for Charu to curtail her imagination along with the expenses involved, no matter what Amal might voice; neither was he much in favour of cost reduction in this manner.

Amal said, "Then, the only other option is to broach Dada with the subject of the garden; he will definitely give us the funds".

"No, what would be the fun and challenge in that? Both of us will develop a garden. He can easily order and have a picturesque one set up – but, what will happen to our plans in that case?"

Amal and Charu were sitting under the shade of the tree and giving full vent to innumerable hopes, plans and dreams. Manda called out from the first floor, "What are you two up to in the garden at such an odd hour?"

"Searching for ripe fruit."

The lascivious Manda immediately said, "If you find any bring some along for me too".

Charu and Amal both laughed. The principal happiness and pride of all their endeavours was the fact that it remained within the confines of only the duo. Manda might be exceptionally gifted in every other way, but imagination was definitely not a quality to be lauded in her. How would she even savour the fun of all these schemes... She was totally exempt from all the committees which these two enlightened members belonged to!

Neither was the estimate of the beloved cherished garden lowered and they found it equally difficult to rein in their imagination. Hence, the committee meetings in the shade of the tree continued for quite some time. Amal carefully demarcated the segments of the garden where the home for the deer, stone edifice etc. would be located.

One fateful day, while Amal was marking with a pickaxe the manner in which the boundary walls of their coveted garden would be constructed, from under the shade of the tree, Charu suddenly spoke, "Amal, it would be wonderful if only you were a writer..."

"Why would it be so wonderful?"

"Then I would request you to compose a story with a description of this garden as the background. This water reservoir, deer house, shady fruit tree, everything would be there – but, except the two of us none could understand the source – it would be great fun. Amal, why don't you try your hand at writing, you will definitely be successful".

Amal answered, "Fine, tell me, if I can write – what will you give me?"

"What do you want?"

"The mosquito net that I use has to be embroidered with eye catching hand drawn decorative."

Charu retorted, "Oh, you are over imaginative! Who has ever heard of a decorative mosquito net?!"

Amal spoke vociferous for making the makeshift nocturnal prison so drab and monotonous. He said, "This is a veritable proof that the majority of people have no sense of beauty and ugliness causes them no discomfort at all".

Charu immediately accepted the logic and in her heart of hearts was thrilled to think that the close committee of only the two of them was not included in that percentage of people. She responded, "Fine, I'll organise the mosquito net – you go ahead and write".

On a note of mystery, Amal remarked, "You think I cannot write?"

Greatly excited Charu burst forth, "That definitely means you have already written something – show me!"

"No, let it be; not today."

"But, it has to be right now – go and fetch your literary output."

It was only an intense desire to show Charu his writing that had held Amal back all this while – suppose Charu did not understand, suppose she did not like what she read! This was a mental block he found it impossible to get rid of.

Presently, bringing forward his notebook and with an embarrassed cough and awkward shuffling the debutante began reading. Leaning against the bark of the tree and stretching out on the green grass Charu began to listen attentively.

The subject matter of the essay was "My Notebook". Amal had waxed eloquent and expressed all his pent up emotions.

Sitting silently beneath the tree Charu listened with rapt attention; then focussing all attention on Amal, she commented, "yet you say you have no literary flair!"

That was the first day Amal imbibed freely of the intoxication of literature; the ambience all around was conducive and the lengthening shadows of the evening appeared to cast mysterious shadows all around.

Charu said, "Amal, some fruits will have to be gathered, or else what will we have to show Manda ..."

The dim-witted Manda was not included in any way to participate in their discussions; hence gathering fruits for her remained the only option.

Chapter 2

Like their innumerable other projects, when the grandiose scheme of their garden petered out in the arena of a limitless imagination, neither Charu nor Amal even noticed.

Presently it was Amal's literary efforts that were the focal point of all their discussions and consultations. Amal might come up and say, "A wonderful idea has just occurred to me..."

In the throes of great enthusiasm Charu would immediately respond, "Let us go to our south verandah – Manda will come here any moment".

Charu would seat herself on a shabby, worn out cane easy-chair and Amal would comfortably sit on the high railing and stretch out his legs.

There was no pattern to the subject matter Amal chose to write about. It was extremely difficult to properly comprehend the complex manner in which he broached a subject. Amal himself would repeatedly comment, "I am just unable to get my message across".

Charu's answer inevitably was, "No indeed, I have understood the most of it – quickly put down what you have told me without any delay".

A mingling of some comprehension, a little lack of understanding and a large amount of imagination instigated an emotional frenzy stimulated by Amal's powers of expression; Charu would thus build up a picture in her mind which would garner her some measure of happiness and bring her to a frenetic point of anticipation.

That very evening Charu would ask, "How far have you progressed?"

"How is that possible in such a short while?"

The next morning on a somewhat quarrelsome note Charu would pounce on him, "So, have you not completed the composition?"

"Just wait a little and let me think farther!"

Angrily Charu would retort, "Then forget it!"

Later, in the evening when Charu's anger reached a point in which all conversation was on the brink of coming to a halt, on the pretext of taking out his handkerchief, Amal would pull out the edge of some paper from his pocket.

In a flash Charu would forget about all vows of silence and gush forth, "There it is – you have written after all! Trying to hoodwink me – come on, show!"

Amal would answer, "It is still not complete, wait a while".

Amal was eager to start there and then; but he never did so till Charu had begged and pleaded for a while. Amal would then take out the bundle of papers and spend some time organising them, taking out a pencil he would proceed to make some corrections; all the while Charu's visage in curious anticipation – like the water laden heavy clouds – would bend low over the papers.

Whether it be one paragraph or two, Amal would have to read aloud to Charu whatever he wrote there and then. The remaining unwritten segment would be discussed between them and imaginatively dissected at length.

All this while both had spun daydreams and now it was turn to harvest poetic meanderings.

One evening when Amal returned from college, it appeared that his pockets were heavier than they usually were. As Amal entered the house, Charu noticed this state of affairs from the inner sanctum of the house.

Usually Amal would not delay entering the house after returning from college; that day he went into the outer room and showed no signs at all of meeting Charu.

Charu came to the entrance of the inner chamber and tried attracting attention by clapping her hands and drawing attention to herself, but all to no avail – no one heard! Angrily Charu retired to the verandah and attempted to immerse herself in a book by Manmatha Dutta.

He was a new author, whose style was somewhat similar to Amal's. Hence Amal was sure never to praise him. Sometimes, with distorted pronunciation he would read aloud from Manmatha Dutta's works and mock him. Charu would inevitably snatch the book from Amal and throw it away.

That day when she finally heard Amal's footsteps approaching, she picked up a copy of his latest book and gave the impression of being engrossed in it.

As Amal entered the verandah, Charu did not even notice. Amal asked, "So, and what are you reading?"

Finding Charu indifferent Amal went behind her and taking note of what she was reading made a rude comment.

Charu said, "Don't bother me now – let me read". Amal started reading in a deliberately imitative fashion and even added a line or two of his own!

Sheer curiosity didn't permit Charu to hold on to her anger. Laughing aloud she cast aside her book and said, "You are extremely jealous and can't stand anybody's writing but your own".

Amal answered, "You are more than generous – the slightest blade of grass and you begin to chew on it".

Charu, "Alright, alright – you need not mock! Just out with what is in your pocket".

"Make a guess as to what it could be."

After irritating Charu for a long time, Amal took out from his pocket the well known journal 'Saroruha'.

Charu noted that Amal's article on the notebook had been published there.

She fell silent. Amal had taken it for granted that Charu would be thrilled. However, not observing any signs of happiness at all he said, "This journal does not publish articles by just anybody".

This statement was somewhat of an exaggeration. If any article passed muster even slightly, the editor did not let it escape him. But, Amal gave Charu to understand that the editor was extremely strict and fussy about the articles he finally chose to be printed.

Charu tried to be pleased at what she heard, but she was unsuccessful. She did try to fathom what had so upset her about this fact, but could find no logical reason at all.

Amal's compositions were property of both – Amal and Charu. One was the writer and the other the reader. It was secrecy that was the prime savour. The fact that all would read it and many would sing praises – Charu could not properly understand why the thought pained her to such a great degree.

Unfortunately the thirst of a writer cannot be quenched by a single reader for a very long time. Amal began to publish his writings and also garnered some praise.

Amal also started receiving fan letters once in a while. He would show them to Charu – the matter would please and yet hurt her at the same time. Now, it no longer remained her sole prerogative to enthuse Amal into writing. Once in a while Amal also began to receive unsigned letters from female readers. Charu would tease him about this, but it definitely did not bring her any great peace. All of a sudden the locked and barred doors of their committee had been thrown wide open and all the enthusiastic and prolific readers of Bengal had stomped in between them.

One day during his leisure hours Bhupati said, "So Charu, I had no idea that our Amal was this adept at writing."

Charu was very pleased at hearing Bhupati praise Amal. Though Bhupati sponsored many young men like Amal, there was a difference between them and this literary artist; when this fact was appreciated Charu blossomed. Her attitude was 'At long last all of you have understood just why I am so fond of Amal. I understood a long time ago that Amal was not one to scoff at ...'"

Charu asked, "Have you read his writing?"

Bhupati answered, "Well... um... not exactly, there has been no time. But our Nishikanta has gone through some and was speaking highly of him. He understands Bengali literature quite well".

Charu greatly desired that feelings of awe and respect for Amal dawned in Bhupati.

Chapter 3

Umapada was explaining to Bhupati about the possibilities of offering other rewards along with the newspaper. It was beyond Bhupati's understanding just how prizes could turn around and make losses into profit.

Entering the room and finding Umapada there, Charu left. Returning again after a while she found both of them engrossed in an argument about accounts.

Noting that Charu was getting impatient, Umapada left on some trumped up pretext. Bhupati began to ponder on the accounts before him.

Entering the room Charu said, "So, your work is not yet over? Sometimes it amazes me how you manage to spend all your time engrossed in the workings of the paper".

Putting aside the accounts, Bhupati smiled. He thought to himself, 'It is regrettably true that not having time for Charu, I neglect her. She has nothing to do to while away her time'.

Affectionately Bhupati remarked, "Today you do not have your studies to occupy you! So, has your teacher taken to his heels? In your school all the rules are topsy turvey – the student is ready with books, but the teacher is not be found! It certainly does not seem that Amal concentrates on your education as he used to do in the past".

Charu said, "Should Amal waste his time teaching me? Do you think that he is no better than a private tutor?"

Tugging on her long braid and drawing her close Bhupati said, "Can teaching someone like you be any ordinary task? If I had someone to teach like you ..."

"Now you don't talk – being a husband is almost more than you can manage and then something more ..."

Somewhat hurt Bhupati continued, "Fine, from tomorrow I will definitely teach you. Bring your books, let me take a look as to what you are studying".

Charu, "That's enough – you don't have to begin with studies! Will you put aside your accounting – at least for the moment? Will you be able to focus on anything else now – tell me that".

"Definitely so! My mind will turn in any direction that you want it to..."

Charu, "That's wonderful – then read through this composition of Amal's and just take note of how outstanding it is. The editor has told Amal that on reading it Nobogopal Babu has said that Amal can easily be called the Ruskin of Bengal".

Hearing such fulsome praise, Bhupati somewhat hesitantly took the writing in hand and took a quick look at the title – 'Monsoon Moon'. For the past two weeks he had been pondering on the budgetary discussions of the Indian Government and his mind was full of this matter. He was mentally absolutely unprepared to read such romantic and pedantic 'Monsoon Moon'. The essay was not short in length either.

After a quick glance through Bhupati scratched his head in puzzlement and remarked, "It's fine, but why me? Is all this within my powers of grasping?"

Awkwardly Charu snatched back the bundle of papers, "Then, what do you understand?"

"I am an ordinary man and understand human beings."

Charu replied, "Then, is literature not about human beings?"

Bhupati, "Such writing is all wrong. Besides, when the man is alive and present in the veritable flesh – where is the necessity of taking recourse to imagination?"

Bhupati then grasped Charulata by the chin and commented, "Just like I understand you, but for me is it necessary to read heavy tomes of literature for that?"

Bhupati took pride in the fact that he did not understand poetry. However, despite not reading Amal's writing, he had developed an innate respect for him. Bhupati would think, 'Though there is nothing to say, the ability to continuously spout forth words takes much more capability than will ever be possible for me. Who would have thought that Amal was so talented!'

While admitting his own paucity in the sphere, Bhupati remained unstinting in his admiration of literature. If a poverty stricken author managed to corner him, he could be inveigled into sponsoring the publication of his book; the only condition was that the book not be dedicated to him. He would buy books and magazines of all genres and sizes and explain it away by, "As it is, I do not read much, if I stop buying too, there will be no end to my sins!" Probably because he did not read them, Bhupati had no animosity at all for sub-standard books, which is one of the reasons why his library overflowed with Bengali books.

Amal would lend a hand in the proof reading of English manuscripts; in order to check some composition with positively horrific handwriting, he hurriedly entered the room.

Bhupati remarked with a smile, "Amal, I have nothing to say at all about any subject you choose to write on, but why curtail my freedom? What kind of torture has Charu planned that she will not let me go without my going through all of them!"

Amal laughed, "How right! If I had known that you would be put through such torture, I would definitely not have written".

In his heart of hearts Amal was very upset with Charu for forcing Bhupati – who was dead against literature – to plod through his precious writings and, immediately realising that, Charu deeply regretted her action. To change the topic of conversation, she said to Bhupati, "Just get your brother married soon – we will then not have to put up with the torture of his writing".

Bhupati said, "Boys of this generation are not as foolish as we were. All their poetry lies in their writing; in their work they are quite adroit. How is it that you have not been able to persuade your brother-in-law to marry?"

Once Charu had left, Bhupati told Amal, "I have to remain involved with all the machinations of the paper and Charu is pretty much left to her own devices. She has no work and once in a while just peers into my office. Tell me, what can I do? If you can keep her occupied with studies, it will be a big help. Sometimes if you read aloud translations of English poetry to her, it will not only be beneficial, but useful to her as well. Charu is quite fond of literature".

"Yes, you are right. I believe that if she were to study a little more, she herself would be quite adept in writing."

Bhupati laughed, "I do not expect so much, but Charu is far better than me in judging Bengali literature".

Amal: "She has a vivid imagination, which is not very common in woman".

Bhupati: "It is not very common amongst men either – I am the living example. Well, if you can develop Charu, I will reward you".

"... and what will that be?"

"I will find a match for you – just like Charu."

Amal: "Then, again I will also have to teach her! Will my entire life go by in such tutoring?!"

Both brothers belonged to the modern generation and there was virtually no seal on their lips.

Chapter 4

Having established himself in the eyes of the readers, Amal was now looking up. Whereas in the past he had been a student, presently he was a stalwart of society. He attended reading sessions and seminars and also had to contend with innumerable invitations. In the eyes of all those who worked in Bhupati's household, he became quite a noteworthy member of the society.

So far Amal had not been worthy of any notice to Mandakini. She would completely disregard his conversations with charu and their earnest literary discussions, preferring to go about her own work. Mandakini would assume that she was by far superior to them and absolutely indispensable to the household.

Amal had an insatiable desire for chewing on betel leaves and it was Manda's responsibility to see that there was a continuous and uninterrupted supply; however, the slightest waste would upset her no end. It was a long standing pastime for Amal and Charu to plunder her stock and this afforded them endless pleasure. But this pleasurable activity afforded Manda no joy at all.

The actual truth of the matter is that a person who has been given shelter does not look on another in a similar position with any degree of favour. The little bit of extra housework that Manda had to do for Amal appeared to her as extremely humiliating. Since Charu was very much in Amal's favour, perforce Manda had to keep her opinion to herself, but the effort to belittle Amal remained ceaseless. In secret she would unhesitatingly speak ill of Amal to the servants – albeit not in his presence. They too would join in.

When Amal's ascent began, Manda was, however, somewhat taken aback. It was no longer the same Amal; his diffident awkwardness was in the past; holding others in contempt appeared to have become his sole prerogative. A man who after gaining a foothold in life without any compunction and hesitation can propagate himself, a man who has gained certain absolute rights, such a man easily attracts the attention of a woman. When Manda found that all were looking up to Amal, she too joined the crowd. The newly gained pride in Amal was the reason behind Manda's growing infatuation. It was as though she came to be newly acquainted with Amal once again.

There was no longer any need to thieve betel leaves; this was yet another loss Charu had to face because of Amal's rise to fame. Their joyous conspiracy was torn asunder. Dressed betel leaves came of their own volition to Amal – there was no longer any need for theft.

Further, the joy and amusement they savoured in keeping Mandakini away from their self – formed group was on the brink of being totally destroyed. It was difficult to keep Manda at a distance. That Amal would consider Charu to be his sole friend, philosopher and guide became intolerable to Manda. She was hell-bent on repaying all former neglect with an abundant surfeit of amiability. Hence, no matter how and when Charu and Amal met, Manda would ensure that she cast the long shadow of her presence over them. There was not even the opportunity to laugh at Manda's sudden volte face.

Needless to say this intrusion was not as bothersome and grating to Amal as to Charu. That an intolerant woman was veering rapidly in his direction definitely was an intoxicant to Amal.

However, observing Manda from a distance, when Charu would comment, "There she comes", Amal too would join in, "Oh no, again the bothersome irritant!" It was a habitual practice with them – to express intolerance for all others; how was it possible for Amal to stop suddenly? Finally when Mandakini had actually come up, Amal would greet her in pretence hospitality.

Manda continued, "Why did you stop abruptly, Amal? I enjoy listening to your output". Prior to this Manda had never expressed any eagerness to further her knowledge – but such a comment would only have caused a further rift.

Charu had no desire that Amal read his latest composition aloud to Manda, but Amal, on the contrary, intensely wanted to... There were many other instances of the sort. Amal recollected yet another incident. Charu and Manda were engrossed in a game when Amal appeared. He was very eager to read aloud to Charu and grew increasingly impatient when the game continued. Finally he spoke, "Then, you'll continue – let me read aloud to Adhir Babu".

Charu firmly clutched at his hand and abruptly ended the game, Manda spoke up, "if you are going to begin your reading session, I will take my leave".

Sheer politeness made Charu offer, "Why don't you stay on and join us?"

"Oh no, I do not understand all this and only feel sleepy." Angry at the rushed end to the game, greatly irritated, Manda left.

That was the same Manda who presently was expressing such eagerness to listen to an excerpt from a literary criticism. Amal responded, "Fine, if you want to listen, that is my good fortune!" Turning the pages, he started right at the beginning – having put in segments which would be attractive, he did not want to miss out on Mandakini's reaction.

Quickly Charu spoke up, "Had you not said that you would be bringing me some old issues of the magazine *Jahnavi* from the library today?"

"No, that was not today."

"Definitely so, then, you have forgotten?"

"Why would I do that? You had said..."

Charu, "Fine, do not bother. You carry on with the reading, I will take my leave; let me send Paresh to the library".

Amal sensed the tension. The matter was apparent to Mandakini and for a few seconds a wave of hatred for Charu rose in her. When Charu had left and Amal was hesitating about whether to break up the session or not, Manda commented with a smile, "Go along my dear, better go and soothe her; Charu is displeased. If you count on me as a listener there will be problems".

After this it became virtually impossible for Amal to leave. Somewhat displeased with Charu, Amal only said, "Why, what's the problem?", and sat back to resume the reading session once again.

Covering both his hands with her own Manda said "There is no need, please do not begin". As if somehow checking her tears, she rapidly left.

Chapter 5

Charu had an outside invitation and Manda was dressing in her room. Calling out loudly Amal abruptly entered the room. Manda was well aware that Amal must have got to hear of Charu's absence due to the invitation. She answered with a smile, "Amal Babu – whom you were searching for and whom you have found! You really are ill-fated!" Adroitly denying and evading the issue, Amal promptly took his seat.

Amal then began, "Tell me about life in your native village and let me listen".

In order to find raw material for his writing, Amal would listen attentively to everything anyone had to say. That was the reason he didn't completely disregard Manda as he had done in the past. Her mentality and history were both of interest to him. Amal began to ask detailed questions about Manda's birth place, village, the manner in which she had spent her childhood and when she had been married etc. Nobody had ever asked such probing questions about Manda's petty and unimportant life. Very happily she continued to prattle on and every once in a while would comment, "I am not even sure what I am talking about..."

Amal further incited her by responding, "No, no – I am enjoying listening, please carry on". Manda at great length and with an equal amount of enjoyment was describing the petty anecdotes which had been slightly out of her mundane and routine daily engagements when Charu suddenly entered.

The story abruptly lost its continuity. It was quite apparent to Charu that her arrival had disrupted a cosy story – telling session.

Amal asked, "How is it that you have returned so early?"

"That is exactly what I am noticing! I have returned much too early". Charu then attempted to take her leave.

Amal persisted, "This is good – you have done me a favour. I was wondering just when you would return. I have brought along a copy of Manmatha Dutta's book to read aloud to you".

Charu, "Let it be for now, I am busy".

Amal, "If there is any work, command me – I will get it done".

Charu was aware that Amal would be bringing along a copy of the book to read aloud to her that day; in order to evoke his envy Charu planned to praise the book profusely – Amal would then read aloud from it in a distorted manner and mock and jibe. Imagining this trend of events Charu had been unable to linger any longer and abruptly putting an end to her invitation on the pretext of sickness had returned home much earlier than planned. Now she bitterly regretted that choice and thought to herself, "I had been much better off there – it was wrong of me to return".

Manda, too, was no less shameless! She sat alone with Amal in a room and bared all her teeth in senseless laughter. What would people say if they caught sight! But it was extremely difficult for Charu to chide Manda for this reason. What if she retorted in like manner? But, there was a vast difference between the two. She enthused Amal in his writing and discussed literature with him; however, that was not Manda's intention in any way. Undoubtedly, Manda wanted to ensnare the simple youth in her coils. It was Charu's duty to rescue Amal from such terrifying and imminent danger. How could she get across to Amal; what this pseudo enchantress' true intentions were? Suppose after understanding, instead of distaste he became further enmeshed?

Charu also felt sorry for her poor brother. He was slogging day and night on her husband's paper while the wife enticed and tried out her wiles on Amal. Charu's brother remained quite at peace as he believed implicitly in his wife. How could Charu remain uninvolved seeing such conjugal unfaithfulness? Terrible!

There had been no problem in the past – it was only since Amal had started writing and attained fame that the crises had loomed large. It was Charu who was the cause of his initiation in literary efforts . What an unfortunate moment it was when she had encouraged him to begin! Did she still retain that influence over Amal as she had in the past? Now Amal had the adulation of many, what difference would it make if one slipped away into nothingness?

It was clear to Charu that great danger would befall if Amal moved away from her world into a domain dominated by others. Amal no longer regarded Charu as his equal – he had grown beyond her. Now, he was an author and Charu merely the reader. Some kind of rectification would have to be made.

Poor simple Amal, enchantress Manda, and misguided duped brother!

Chapter 6

Early monsoon clouds had overcast the sky. As it was dark in the room Charu was sitting by the open window and bending low, writing something with absolute concentration.

She did not even come to know when Amal approached and stood behind her. In the soft soothing light Charu continued to write and Amal continued to read; besides lay scattered a couple of Amal's printed works. They were Charu's only models for writing.

"Then, how is it that you say you cannot write!"

Unexpectedly hearing Amal's voice Charu was greatly startled. Quickly hiding her notebook she said, "This is very wrong of you!"

"... and what is this misdemeanour?"

"Why were you sneakily reading what I had written?"

"... simply because it was impossible to do so openly."

Charu quickly tried to shred what she had written. Amal just as rapidly snatched the notebook from her hands. Charu said, "If you read what has been written, I will stop talking to you all my life".

Amal retorted, "If you ask me not to, then I will not talk to you all my life".

Although Charu begged and pleaded, ultimately she had to give in. The reason was simple – she was longing to show her writing to Amal and yet had not realised that she would feel so awkward actually doing so. When, by dint of begging and pleading, Amal began to read, Charu felt as though she were freezing with embarrassment. On a trumped up excuse, she quickly left the room.

On completion Amal went up to Charu and said, "It is excellent".

Charu forgot what she was allegedly engrossed in and said, "What nonsense! You don't have to tease me... Please return my copy".

Amal answered, "No, I won't do that now – I will copy the matter and send it for publication".

"Send it indeed – no!"

Charu began to raise a great deal of fuss. Amal too remained adamant. He repeatedly swore, "It is definitely fit to be sent for publication," and Charu found no other option but to say in a resigned manner, "There is no controlling when you make up your mind about something!"

Amal went on, "This must be shown to Dada".

At that Charu threw aside what she was doing and stood up. She once again tried to snatch away her copy and said, "No, you cannot read aloud my composition to him. If you do that I will not write a word again".

Amal, "You are mistaken on your attitude. No matter what Dada, my elder brother, might say, he will be thrilled at seeing your writing".

"No matter, there is no need for such thrills."

Charu had promised that she would write and amaze Amal; she would not stop before proving that there was a world of difference between Manda and herself. The past few days she had written prolifically and torn up what she had written. Whatever she wanted to write became rather similar to Amal's compositions and some a veritable copy! Those were the ones that were good, the others were extremely immature. Out of fear that Amal would laugh, Charu tore the writings into shreds and threw them into the pond so that even by chance Amal did not get to lay his hands on them. When she had begun writing, she found to her dismay that even the rhyming couplets were sounding extremely similar.

Finding it virtually impossible to avoid Amal's literary influence, Charu changed the subject matter of her writing altogether. She wrote an essay, entitling it after the temple dedicated to the Goddess Kali in her native village. The descriptions centred on the emotions – fear mingled with devotion and curiosity that this structure evoked. Initially Amal's influence could be clearly made out, but later Charu found her own niche and style.

Amal grabbed this writing, reading it attentively. In his opinion, the beginning was quite poetic, but towards the end Charu had not been able to maintain the same pace and style. Anyway, for a first effort, the composition was extremely laudable.

Charu said, "What do you say to the publication of a monthly journal?"

"Unless there is a fair bit of money involved, how is the publication going to be sustained?"

Charu, "But there are absolutely no expenses involved. After all it will not be published – it will be hand-written. Thus there will be contributions only by both of us and there will be none other to read it either. One will be for you and one for me".

Even a few days ago Amal would have enthusiastically leaped up at this idea; now, he no longer felt as enamoured of the idea of secrecy. He no longer felt any pleasure unless his writing was read by one and all. However, to maintain the facade of the past, he expressed his support saying, "That will be a lot of fun".

Charu continued, "But, you will have to promise that besides our paper, the writing will not be published elsewhere".

"But then the editors are going to slaughter us!"

Charu, "... and do you think that there are no weapons of destruction with me?"

A decision was thus reached and a committee set up consisting of two editors, two writers and two readers. Amal suggested, "Let the name of the paper be '*CHARUPAATH*' – *the reading Charu*. But Charu insisted, "No, it should be *AMALA*". The new arrangements made Charu forget her sorrows and problems for a few days. After all, there was no way Manda could gain entrance into this world of their monthly journal and the doors remained barred to all outsiders too.

Chapter 7

One day Bhupati said, "Charu, there was never any decision that you would turn into an author!"

Charu blushed in embarrassment, "I, an author! Who has told you this? Never!"

"Proof is ready and waiting!" Bhupati then proceeded to take out a bundle of the journal *"Saroruha"*. Charu then discovered that everything she had taken for granted was to be their secret hoard had been neatly gathered and published along with their names in the said journal.

Charu felt as though someone had without permission released favourite pet birds from their cages. Forgetting her embarrassment at being caught out by Bhupati, anger rapidly escalated against Amal.

"Just take a look at this one!" Opening yet another newspaper, Bhupati held it out to Charu. There was an article dealing with the modern trends of prose writing.

Charu pushed it aside and her feelings of hurt as regards Amal grew by leaps and bounds. Bhupati, however, forced her to continue reading.

Charu had no option but to continue going through the bit of writing. The contributor of the piece had written scathingly about the wordy and pedantic style of writing about a certain segment of modern prose writers. Amongst them the author sharply jibed Amal and Manmatha Dutta's compositions; alongside he had compared the writing of the new and upcoming authoress Charubala's unadorned simplicity, easy flow of language, and skilful use of words in drawing pictures. He had further written that only if such a style were followed could there be any hope of redemption for Amal or else there was no doubt that they would fail completely.

Bhupati commented with a style, "This is what is called the student overtaking the teacher!"

About to take pleasure in this first praise of her writing, Charu almost immediately felt an acute pain. Her heart seemed absolutely reluctant to be joyous in any manner. About to imbibe of the chalice of praise, she dashed it to the ground once again.

It was clear to her that Amal had intended to catch her completely in surprise by having her article published in the paper. When it was finally published and when some favourable reviews had appeared, he would both appease and further stimulate her interest. When the praise actually appeared, why did Amal not appear with true enthusiasm? The truth was that Charu's praise hurt him, which is why he had hidden the paper and kept it a secret for as long as possible. The little nest of comfort that Charu had built up through her own writing was suddenly shattered by a virtual onslaught of praise. Charu did not find this pleasing in the least.

When Bhupati left, Charu remained sitting in silence on the bed; the journals were open in front of her.

Notebook in hand Amal entered silently, intending to catch Charu by surprise. He drew close to find her engrossed in one of the literary criticisms that had been published.

Just as silently Amal tiptoed out of the room. 'Merely because I have been abused and she herself praised, Charu is not even conscious or aware of anything else.' In a flash his entire being flooded with a strange bitterness. Amal firmly decided that Charu's ego had spiralled beyond all recognition and the anger in him steadily grew. The right reaction would have been to shred the paper into bins immediately and burn them to cinder.

Angry with Charu, Amal went to Manda's room and loudly called out for her. Manda greeted him with effusive hospitality.

Amal, "Would you like to listen to an excerpt from my new composition?"

"You have been promising me for a number of days now, but the promise has just not materialised. No matter, there is no need; there might be people who will be angered and that would cause problems for you. What difference does it make to me?"

Somewhat sharply Amal responded, "Who would be angry and for what reason? Never mind, that will be tackled. For the moment, you can be my audience".

As if with extreme eagerness Manda sat up attentively. Amal, with due fanfare, began his impromptu reading session.

This was truly foreign matter for Manda, she had no concept at all of what Amal was talking about. It was for that very reason that she gave the impression of absorbed attention and excessive enthusiasm. In full spate Amal's voice began to rise proportionately.

As Amal was in full swing, a shadow fell across Manda's threshold. Manda noticed, but ignoring it started listening to Amal with even more rapt attention.

Instantly the shadow vanished.

Charu had been waiting for Amal – so that the journal could be soundly berated; she would also get a chance to castigate Amal for breaking his promise not to have any of her writing published, except in their own journal.

The time for Amal's visit came and went by. Charu had chosen a composition for Amal to hear – that too lay neglected at one corner.

All of a sudden Charu seemed to hear the echo of Amal's voice from somewhere in the house – and it seemed to be Manda's room! Like one mortally wounded she got up and silently stood outside Manda's room. Charu had not heard what Amal was reading aloud to Manda.

Charu found it impossible to return as silently as she had arrived. The three consecutive blows she had received that day made her lose all semblance of patience. She felt like screaming aloud that Manda's total incomprehension and Amal's lunacy in reading aloud to her was only too apparent. However, not speaking, stomping her way back loudly, she made her displeasure abundantly clear. Entering her bedroom, Charu emphatically locked her door.

Amal paused in his reading for a bit and, laughing, Manda indicated Charu's fleeting presence. Amal thought to himself, "What kind of tyranny is this? Charu seems to have decided that I am her pet slave and cannot read aloud to anyone but her". Keeping this in mind, he started reading at an even louder pitch.

On completion, he left, passing by Charu's room. Taking a quick glance he found the door locked.

From the sound of footsteps Charu made out that Amal was passing by her room and not pausing even for a few minutes. She felt like weeping in hurt and humiliation. Taking out her new notebook, she tore the pages into tiny little bits, making a small heap. Alas! What an evil moment it had been when she had started writing...

Chapter 8

In the evening the fragrance of the jasmine flowers wafted across from the garden. From between scattered clouds in a serene sky the stars glistened brightly. That day neither had Charu changed, nor had she dressed; she remained sitting alone by the window in darkness. The wind blew through her open tresses and tears flowed down her eyes in such a manner that she was not even aware herself.

At such a juncture Bhupati entered the room – heavy hearted and face downcast. It was not the usual time for him to return. Normally after overseeing all the activities of the paper and retiring for the day, it was quite late by the time he returned home. That evening, as if in expectation of some solace from Charu, he returned much earlier.

No lamps had been lit in the room. Through the light streaming in from the open window Bhupati could indistinctly make out Charu sitting there in solitude; slowly he came and stood by her. Despite hearing footsteps she did not look around and remained sitting – still and unmoving.

Somewhat astonished Bhupati called out, "Charu!"

At Bhupati's voice, Charu sat up abruptly. She had not even guessed that it could be Bhupati returning.

Very affectionately running his fingers through Charu's hair Bhupati asked, "How is it that you are sitting alone in the dark? Where is Manda?"

That day nothing had gone the way Charu had expected. She had definitely assumed that Amal would return and ask for forgiveness – that was what she had been waiting for. Bhupati's sudden arrival tore asunder her self-control and she burst into tears.

Pained, Bhupati hurriedly queried, "Charu, what's the matter?"

It was difficult to pinpoint what exactly was wrong. After all, what was the matter? Nothing momentous had occurred. Instead of her, Amal had read aloud his writing to Manda first – what kind of complaint could she make to Bhupati about that? Wouldn't he laugh? It was impossible for Charu to identify the true nature of her pain and discomfort in the midst of such a petty incident. Unable to understand just why she was in so much agony for practically no reason at all, the pain increased manifold times.

Bhupati sympathetically said "Tell me Charu, what is the matter? Have I done you any injustice? You are just very aware of how complex and time consuming my work with the newspaper is – if I have hurt you in any way, it has been absolutely unintentional".

Bhupati was asking such questions which had no answers and served only to make Charu innately more restless; all she felt was – if only he gave her some respite – that was all she was looking for...drenched with affection.

Not getting any answer for the second time, Bhupati once again asked in soft tones, "It is impossible to be with you for any length of time, Charu – but that will not happen any longer. Henceforth my paper will not occupy my attention all the time. You will get as much of me as you desire".

Impatiently Charu spoke up, "No, that is not the reason".

Bhupati went on, "Then what's the reason?". He sat down firmly on the bed.

Unable to hide her irritation any longer Charu said, "Let it be for now, I will tell you at night".

Remaining silent for a few minutes Bhupati said, "Fine, then let it be". He proceeded to leave the room without saying anything further. What he had come to say remained unsaid.

It was no secret to Charu that Bhupati was passing through some kind of emotional crisis and for a flash thought about calling him back. A searing regret passed through her, but she could not find any means of retrieval.

With the fall of night, Charu took great care over Bhupati's dinner and sat down to fan him.

All of a sudden she heard Manda call out loudly, "Braja... Braja". When he answered, she asked, "Has Amal Babu had his meal?" – to which the answer was in the affirmative. Manda then proceeded to thoroughly berate the servant for not ensuring that betel leaves were dressed and immediately handed to him.

Charu had resolved that on that day she would talk gently and pleasantly to Bhupati and have an enlivening conversation. But Manda's voice shoved aside all her plans and she found it impossible to say even a word to Bhupati while he ate. Bhupati too also remained rather gloomy and depressed. He could not eat properly. Charu just asked him once, "Why have you lost your appetite?"

Bhupati protested, "Why? I am eating as I always do ..."

When both were in the bedroom Bhupati asked, "You were going to tell me something tonight?"

Charu answered, "Manda's demeanour and manner leave me concerned and I am no longer comfortable about having her here".

"Why? What has she done?"

"She behaves so familiarly with Amal that it is positively embarrassing."

Bhupati laughed aloud, "Oh no! This is lunacy. Amal is just a young lad!"

Charu, "This is just like you. You keep no information about what is happening at home and are acquainted only with news of the outside world. Anyway, my sympathies are with my poor brother. Manda keeps no track at all of whether or not my brother has his meals properly; but, should there be anything even slightly amiss with Amal's food, she does not hesitate to soundly take the servants to task".

Bhupati murmured, "You women are extremely suspicious by nature ..."

Angrily Charu retorted, "That may be or not, but this kind of debauchery cannot continue in my home, let me warn you".

· Bhupati was somewhat amused at these baseless reservations, but was a little pleased at the same time. There was a strange kind of sweetness in the excessive wariness and qualms that women battled against in order to preserve the sanctity of their household.

In pride and affection Bhupati kissed Charu on the forehead and said, "There is no need to create any further furore about this; Umapada is leaving for Mymensingh to set up his practice there and will be taking Manda along".

Finally, in order to do away with his own worries and put an end to this kind of unsavoury discussion, Bhupati picking up Charu's notebook said, "Why don't you read aloud from your writings to me, Charu?"

She immediately snatched back the book, "You will not like this and only laugh at me".

Bhupati was a little hurt at this, but hid it with a smile and said, "Not at all; as a matter of fact, I will listen sitting so still that you might even think I have fallen asleep!"

However, Bhupati could not manage to convince Charu – in no time the copy and all other materials disappeared beneath a pile of mundane household articles.

Chapter 9

Bhupati had found it impossible to confide his inner turmoil Charu. Umapada was the chief of Bhupati's newspaper operation – he was responsible for all the expenses involved in running the journal. All of a sudden, Bhupati was astounded and shocked to get a letter from a lawyer on behalf of the newspaper – apparently he owed them a fairly substantial amount of money. Bhupati sent for Umapada and asked the reason since the money for the payment had already been given to him.

Umapada answered, "They must have made some kind of mistake".

However, facts could no longer remain hidden. Umapada had been siphoning off money in this manner for a very long time. Not merely that, he had also borrowed money in Bhupati's name from a large number of people. He had constructed a permanent house in his village and the better part of all the payments had been made from funds intended for Bhupati's newspaper.

When Umapada was cornered and had to own up, he said aggressively, "It is not that I am about to abscond. Gradually all the money will be repaid. I am not worthy of being addressed by my own name if even a single paise remains due".

None of it made any difference to Bhupati. It was not even the loss of money that greatly upset him; this sudden and unexpected betrayal made him feel as though he had suddenly stepped into space, with no support below.

That was the day he had untimely gone to the inner sanctum. His heart hankered to feel – even momentarily – that one place in the universe where there was implicit trust and faith. At that time, immersed in her own sorrows, Charu had been sitting in silence in the darkness, in front of the window.

The very next day Umapada was prepared to leave for Mymensingh. He wanted to make himself scarce before all the creditors came to know of his movement. Sheer disgust prevented

Bhupati from even talking to Umapada when he left. The latter, however, regarded this silence as supreme good fortune.

Amal came and asked, "And what is this that is happening? What is this sudden spree of packing all about?"

Manda replied, "Oh, well, one would have to leave some time – is it possible to remain here forever?"

"Where are you going?"

"To our village – home."

"Why, what was the problem here?"

Manda continued piteously, "Tell me, have I ever complained about any problem? I was happy enough to spend my days with all of you. But this is beginning to cause problems for certain people," saying which she looked suggestively in the direction of Charu's room.

Amal remained gravely silent. Manda went on, "Shame! Shame! What Babu must have thought".

Amal did not waste time on further discussions on this subject. However, he wondered about whatever Charu had communicated to her husband about the relationship between him and Manda.

Emerging from the house Amal began to wander about the streets. He did not feel like returning to the house. If his brother believed Charu's insinuations and assumed his guilt he would have no other option, but to take the same kind of decision as Manda. In a manner of speaking, Manda's banishment also meant expulsion for Amal – it was just that the order had not been verbalised so far – no question of staying here any further. However, neither was it possible to allow his brother to nurture such a wrong impression. So long, he had with implicit trust given him shelter and brought him up. How could he possibly leave without making it absolutely clear to his brother that his trust had not been betrayed in any way at all.

At the time Bhupati was sitting overburdened with thoughts of a relative's betrayal, being harried by creditors, trumped up accounts and a virtually empty treasury. There was none to share this sorrow with him – Bhupati was mentally gearing himself to prepare for a solitary battle in the future.

Amal suddenly entered the room in a flurry. Deeply absorbed in his own thoughts, Bhupati looked up with a start and asked, "well, what is the news Amal?"

For a moment he thought, it seemed to him that Amal too had come with news of some calamity.

Amal said, "Dada, have I ever given you any cause to suspect me in any manner?"

Amazed Bhupati asked, "Suspect you!" He brooded in his heart of hearts, 'With all that is happening, I won't be surprised if I have to start suspecting even Amal".

Amal: "Have you received any complaints about my character from Charu Bouthan?"

Bhupati thought, "Oh, so that is what the matter is! Thank God! It is a hurt engendered by affection. He had thought that it was just one major problem following another. But, even during times of grave crisis, attention has to be paid to petty problems like this too.

At any other time Bhupati would have teased Amal about the alleged complaint, but presently his frame of mind was not such that it could tolerate any degree of jocularity. He merely commented, "Have you turned insane or what!"

Amal asked once again, "Has Charu Bouthan not said anything?"

"If out of love for you she has said something, there is absolutely no cause for anger."

Amal: "Now the time has come for me to seek some kind of work elsewhere."

At that Bhupati soundly scolded him, "Amal, is there no end to your childishness? Now focus on your studies, a job can come later".

Depressed Amal walked away, Bhupati sat down to tally detailed accounts once again.

Chapter 10

Amal decided that some sort of closure would have to be made to this discord – there was no other option to a confrontation. He began to reiterate in his own mind all the harsh words that he would address to Charu.

After Manda had left, Charu decided that she herself would send for Amal and by some means or the other appease him. But he would have to be summoned on the pretext of some writing. She had written an essay based on Amal's style of writing and subject matter. It was abundantly clear to Charu that Amal did not appreciate her independent style of writing.

On the other hand, the third member of the family, Bhupati, had gone to his friend Motilal for advice on how to free himself from imminent danger by meeting his debts.

Bhupati had lent this friend some money and, finding no other viable option, very hesitantly approached him for repayment. Motilal was relaxing under the cool breeze of the fan after his bath and praying to the Almighty with wholehearted concentration. On seeing Bhupati he greeted him with effusive cordiality.

When the question of repayment of money came up, he gave the matter a lot of thought and then asked in amazement, "What money would you be referring to? Have you lent me anything in the recent past?"

In all innocence, Bhupati specified the detail, to which his friend responded, "Oh, but that has been repaid a long time ago!"

In a flash, everybody all around Bhupati changed diametrically. The segment of society which was unmasked before his very eyes made him shudder in horror. During times of flood, just as those in distress rush to the highest point for shelter, instinct drove Bhupati straight to the inner sanctum of his own home. He thought to himself, "No matter who else, Charu will never let me down".

Charu was then seated on her bed and bending over industriously writing into her notebook. It was only when Bhupati actually went and took his seat beside her that she heeded his presence. Immediately she hid the book into which she had been writing.

When the heart is vulnerable, even the slightest blow hurts manifold times. The rapidity with which Charu hid her book grievously wounded Bhupati's sensibility.

Slowly Bhupati took his place beside Charu on the bed. Somewhat awkward at the sudden interruption and the scurried effort to hide her book forbade Charu to utter even a single word in embarrassed discomfiture.

That day Bhupati had nothing to say or even ask for himself. Bare handed and totally bereft he had come to Charu as a supplicant. If she had been even a little concerned and worried about his welfare and shown a bit of affection, it would have been a great salve to his wounds.

Unfortunately a momentary need had robbed Charu of all words and she remained cloaked in an unapproachable silence.

After sitting in silence for a while Bhupati sighed deeply and without a word got up from the bed and left the room.

That was the time when Amal, armed with a string of harsh expletives, was rapidly approaching Charu's room; midway espying Bhupati looking so wan and disturbed, Amal came to an abrupt halt. He could not help asking, "Dada, are you not well?"

Hearing Amal's calm and loving tones, Bhupati's heart seemed to swell with all the accumulated unshed tears. For some time there was no conversation at all. Exerting all his will power, Bhupati restrained himself and said "Nothing is wrong. So, Amal, will there be any writing from you in this issue of the journal?"

The impending tirade vanished into nothingness. Amal quickly approached Charu's room and asked anxiously, "What is the matter with Dada?"

"There is nothing that I could make out. Perhaps the other newspapers have abused his journal."

Amal shook his head.

The fact that Amal had come without being called and that he was conversing perfectly normally brought Charu a deep sense of relief. Straightaway she broached the subject of her writing, "Today, I was on the brink of writing something new – and he almost caught me at it!"

Charu had been sure that Amal would plead to have a look and covertly she even moved the copy about a bit. However, Amal once gazed sharply and searchingly at Charu and continued to remain silent. Abruptly he got up. Sometimes, while traversing a mountainous path, thanks to a sudden and unexpected flash of lightening, the unwary traveller comes to realise that he had been on the brink of falling into a deep ravine. Not making any kind of response, Amal silently left the room.

Amal's strange and abrupt response remained totally incomprehensible to Charu.

Chapter 11

The next day Bhupati once again entered the bedroom at an untimely hour and sent for Charu and said, "Quite a good proposal has come for Amal".

Charu was somewhat absent-minded and commented, "What's this good proposal?"

"It's proposal for marriage."

"Why, was I not good enough?"

Bhupati laughed aloud uproariously, "I am yet to ask Amal whether or not he liked you. Even if he did, I have some sort of a prior claim and do not intend to let go of it so easily".

Charu, "Oh! There is no stopping you from making these most banal remarks. Didn't you say that a marriage proposal had come for you?" Charu's face flushed with embarrassment.

Bhupati: "Then, would I have come running to inform you? There would not even be the hope of being rewarded".

Charu: "So a proposal has come asking for Amal's hand in marriage? Then no delay makes any sense."

Bhupati: "The lawyer Raghunath Babu from Burdwan wants Amal to marry his daughter and then send him overseas for higher studies.

Charu was stunned, "Overseas?!"

"Yes, England."

"Amal will go to England? That is going to be fun. This is a very good idea – have you talked the matter over with him?"

Bhupati: "Instead of me, won't it be better if you have a word with him and broach the subject first?"

Charu: "I have told him a million times, but he refuses to listen to me. I cannot speak to him."

"Do you then think that he will not agree?"

"A number of efforts have also been made at other times, but so far he has not agreed."

Bhupati: "But it would be unwise of him to let go of the proposal this time. I have incurred a lot of debts and it is becoming impossible for me to sponsor Amal as I have done in the past".

Bhupati sent for Amal and on his arrival said, "Raghunath Babu of Burdwan has proposed a marriage between his daughter and you. He desires to send you overseas. What is your opinion?"

Amal answered, "If you have no objection, I'm agreeable to the proposal".

Amal's answer surprised both immeasurably. None had thought that he would agree as soon as he was asked.

Charu could not help jeering, "The lad will agree as soon as his brother gives permission! What impressive obedience! Where has it been all this while, my dear?"

Instead of speaking, Amal merely smiled a bit.

As if to forcibly elicit some sort of a reaction from him, Charu commented even more venomously, "Instead, why don't you admit that your interest has been aroused? Where was the need to pretend all this while that you were not interested in marrying? There is the hunger to marry, but embarrassment at coming out into the open".

Bhupati also teased, "Amal had kept his desire undercover all this while so that you would not be jealous of your sister-in-law!"

Charu flared up at this and spoke vociferously, "Envy! Indeed! There can never be any question of jealousy. It is very wrong of you to speak in this manner".

Bhupati: "Now look at that, doesn't a man even have the right to tease his own wife?"

"No, I do not like such jokes."

"Alright, it is a grievous sin that I have committed. Forgive me. However, are you agreeable to the marriage?"

Amal replied in the affirmative.

Charu: "So, you cannot even wait to go and verify at least once just what kind of girl she is. Not once did you reveal that matters have come to such a pass".

Bhupati: "Amal, if you so desire, arrangements can be made to take a look at the girl. I have made enquiries and believe that she is quite good looking".

Amal, "No, I don't see the necessity".

Charu: "Why do you listen to him? Is such a decision possible? Is it possible to get him married without taking a look at the prospective bride? If he is not interested, we can go over".

Amal, "No Dada, there is no need for any kind of unnecessary delay".

Charu: "No, no – there is no need – any delay will shatter him to pieces. Why not dress and set out for the marriage right now? Just suppose if someone else intervenes and whisks her away!"

None of Charu's jibes had, however, any effect on Amal.

Charu: "Then, your mind is panting to leave for England? Why, were we mistreating you here in any manner? These days, unless accoutred like a sahib, young men are just not satisfied. Will you be able to even recognise us after returning from England?"

Amal answered, "Then, what is the use of going to England?"

Bhupati laughed, "It is to forget the dark form that this journey overseas is being organised. Why be afraid Charu? We are all left behind – there won't be lack of any dark people to worship".

Happily Bhupati sent a letter to Burdwan immediately. The date of the marriage was fixed.

Chapter 12

In the meanwhile, the paper had to be wound up. Bhupati found it impossible to meet expenses any longer. Bhupati had to give up in a flash the public he had spent all these years wooing. The main stream along which Bhupati's life had been moving in a pattern all these twelve years all of a sudden was thrown at the deep end of the water. Bhupati was absolutely unprepared for such a change. All the enthusiasm and efforts of so many years – where would he now find a diversion? Like hungry orphan children they all seemed to look up at Bhupati and he in turn brought them along and presented them to the lady bountiful in his own home.

The lady was then immersed in thoughts of her own. She wondered, 'What is so surprising? It is very good that Amal is getting married. But after all these years, that he is leaving us and getting married in another household, does it not make him hesitate even a little? All the care that we have lavished on him all this while; no sooner did an opportunity present itself than he immediately began making preparations? It seems this is just what he has been waiting for all this while. But on the face of it there was so much sweetness, so much love. There is no way one can recognise people. Who would have guessed that a man who can write so prolifically has an empty heart?"

Comparing Amal's empty heart to her own overfull one, Charu tried to look down on him, but found it impossible to do so. From her innermost being shafts of pain began to push her hurt to the fore, 'Amal would be leaving within a short while, but he did not even bother about coming to meet her. The chasm had opened between them – he did not find the time even to try to cross it and make the wounds heal'. Charu constantly thought that Amal would remember all their youthful follies and games and come over surely as he could not sever ties so abruptly. But no, Amal did not come. Finally, when the day of departure drew absolutely close, Charu herself sent for Amal.

Amal answered, "I will go a little later". Charu went and took her seat on their familiar spot on the verandah. Since the morning thick clouds had made it ominously sultry; her tresses open and untrammelled, Charu sat wearily by the window and gently began to fan herself.

It grew late. Gradually, her movements became sloth and the fan stopped moving. Rage, hurt and impatience began to shatter her equanimity and she said to herself, 'What does it matter if Amal does not come?' Even then, no sooner were footsteps heard than she would start and look around.

A distant church clock struck eleven. Bhupati would be arriving for his meal in no time; there was still half an hour to hope and wait for Amal's arrival. Somehow or the other their silent discord of the past few days would have to be resolved – she could not possibly bid farewell to Amal in this manner. This sweet relationship that existed between sister and brother-in-law of the same age – so much bonding and so many emotional ties, Amal would be severing them all and leaving for some faraway country. Would he not repent even a little? Would even the last tears not moisten their relationship?

The half hour was almost over. Charu restlessly fidgeted as she waited – it was becoming impossible to restrain her tears any longer. The servant came to ask for instructions. Charu answered rather tersely and abruptly – surprised, the man left without saying anything further.

Some strong emotion began to push upwards and clog Charu's throat.

At the usual time Bhupati, smiling, came to have his dinner. Charu found that Amal had accompanied her husband. She did not even look at him.

Amal asked, "Had you sent for me?"

Charu answered, "No, there is no longer any need".

"Then let me take my leave now, there is a lot of organising that remains to be done."

Charu just once gazed at Amal and said tersely, "Sure, go!"

Amal, too looked up and left.

At the end of the meal Bhupati was in the habit of sitting by Charu for a while. However, that day being extremely busy with sorting out accounts, he could not spend much time and, hence, a little upset, remarked, "Today I cannot spend much time with you – there are lots of complications".

"So, just leave!"

Bhupati thought that Charu was upset and responded, "That doesn't mean I have to leave immediately – definitely I will have to rest for a while". As he sat down he noticed that Charu was somewhat depressed. Penitently, Bhupati remained by her side for a long while, but just could not break the ice. After trying futilely to converse, ultimately he gave up and said, "Amal will be leaving tomorrow, probably you will feel very lonely for a few days".

Instead of answering Charu quickly left the room on the pretext of fetching something. Bhupati waited for a while and then left.

Looking up at Amal that day Charu had noticed that he had grown very thin – that youthful vigour was not present. This saddened Charu and yet made her glad at the same time. Charu was in no doubt at all that it was their imminent parting that was the reason behind Amal losing weight; but why did he persist in behaving in this manner? Why did he continue to keep a safe distance? Why did he make their parting so emotionally disruptive?

Lying in bed and thinking of all this, Charu sat up abruptly – she had remembered Manda. If it so happened that Amal loved Manda ... If it was because Manda had left that Amal – shame! Could Amal really think in such a manner? Could it be so petty and tainted? Could he fall in love with a married woman? Impossible. Charu forcibly tried to push away all suspicions, but it continued to firmly hold her in its grasp.

In this manner the day of departure came. The clouds did not clear. Amal came and said in trembling tones, "It is time for me to leave. Henceforth please take good care of Dada. He is contending with a grave crisis now – there is none but you to offer him consolation".

Taking note of Bhupati's wan and melancholic demeanour, Amal had investigated and found out about the crisis he was facing. The manner in which Bhupati was contending with this manner of calamity all alone, not receiving any help or solace from anybody – but, not for an instance did he allow all those who depended on him to be disturbed in any way; thinking of all this Amal remained silent. Then he pondered on Charu, on himself, his ears grew warm; he thought to himself, "Forget all manner of creative writing; if I can return as a barrister and support Dada – only then can I call myself a man".

The entire previous night Charu had spent brooding on what she would tell Amal at the moment of parting. She had practised her words to take on both hurt and joy; but at the actual moment of parting, Charu found she could not speak a word. She only said, "You will write, won't you, Amal?"

Amal took his leave and Charu – running to her bedroom – locked the door.

Chapter 13

Bhupati, having travelled to Burdwan for Amal's marriage waited till the completion of the ceremonies and returned after seeing Amal off to England.

Being hurt on so many fronts, the normally trusting Bhupati felt a kind of uninvolved ennui with the outside world. Meetings, committees – nothing appealed to him any longer. The one recurring thought to him was, "All this while I have been merely deceiving myself by remaining involved with all these activities. The best years of my life have thus gone by and wasted – no better than garbage".

Bhupati continued to think, "Well, it's good that the paper has gone – I am now free". Just as when dusk falls, birds flock home at the first sign of darkness, Bhupati, discarding his habit of so many years, unerringly made his way to Charu. He firmly decided, "Enough is enough – now, my entire world will be within these boundaries. The paper boat of my newspaper has been scuttled – now it is time for me to return home".

Bhupati probably held on to the concept that no one gave a husband rights over his wife; it was by virtue of her own wifely characteristic that she shone forth like the guiding star. Any test or proof was redundant – when everything was breaking all around,

Bhupati felt not the slightest urge to test the bastions of his own little kingdom.

Bhupati returned home from Burdwan in the evening; he washed quickly and had his meal. Firmly believing that Charu was eagerly waiting to hear the details of the wedding and all about Amal's departure for England, Bhupati did not waste any time at all. In the bedroom, Bhupati lay back, puffing luxuriously on the tobacco-pipe. Charu was not present at the time – in all likelihood busy with housework. Bhupati began to feel sleepy and, as moments went by, sometimes he would wake up with a start and wonder just why Charu was not putting in an appearance. Finally, unable to wait any longer, Bhupati sent for her and asked, "How is it that you are so late today?"

Charu merely agreed, "Yes, it is rather late".

Bhupati awaited Charu's eager questions; but she asked nothing at all. That upset Bhupati. Then, was Charu not fond of Amal? All the time that Amal had spent with them, there was no end to all the concern and worry for him, but no sooner had he left than there was complete disregard! This kind of contradictory, unseemly and unfeminine behaviour sounded a false note. He began to wonder – then, was Charu a shallow woman? Did she appreciate only amusement and not know how to love? It was not good for a woman to be so dispassionate and uninvolved.

Bhupati had enjoyed Charu's and Amal's friendship. There was a curious charm in their amity, their fights and quarrels and making up. The manner in which Charu took such tender care of Amal pleased Bhupati no end – highlighting her soft and gentle womanly qualities. Now he wondered with amazement – then, were all those feelings without any substance or foundation? Bhupati reflected – if Charu had no heart at all, how could he himself expect to find a home, a shelter?

To test the waters Bhupati broached the subject, "Charu, have you been keeping well? You are not ill?"

The terse answer came, "I am alright".

"Amal's wedding is over."

Bhupati then fell silent; no matter how hard Charu tried, she could not bring herself to put forward any relevant query about what had happened. She remained tense and alert.

By nature Bhupati was somewhat obtuse; but, being pained at Amal's departure, Charu's disinterest hurt him. He had wanted to discuss the matter with Charu, and, as a fellow sufferers, both could console each other.

Bhupati, "The girl is quite pretty. – Charu, are you sleeping?"

"No."

Bhupati, "Poor Amal all alone. When I saw him off in the car, he wept helplessly like a child – at that, I could not control my tears, even at this age. There were two sahibs in the compartment – they were extremely amused at the sight of two grown men weeping".

In the dark room, Charu first of all turned to one side and then rapidly left the room. Startled Bhupati asked, "Charu, are you sick?"

Not finding any answer, Bhupati too got up. Hearing the sound of muffled tears from the verandah, he found Charu on the floor, desperately trying to stem the weeping that was threatening to overwhelm her.

The sight of so much searing pain astounded Bhupati. How badly I misunderstood Charu – she is naturally so reticent that even with me she hesitates to share her agony. Those who are similarly introvert love deeply and feel sorrow just as intensely. It became apparent to Bhupati that Charu's love was not as obvious as that of the average woman. He had never witnessed the throes of Charu's love; presently it was only too clear to him that her love was prolific internally. Bhupati himself was not very expressive. Finding the concrete manifestation of Charu's deep emotions greatly reassured him.

Bhupati silently stood by Charu and gently began to pat her. He did not know how to console; however, what he did not understand was that when one wanted to smother this intensity of sorrow, any witness was most unwanted.

Chapter 14

When Bhupati took leave from the newspaper, he had drawn a clear picture in his own mind about his future. He had firmly resolved not to enter into any kind of strained effort for no matter what ... His life would henceforth consist of enjoyment of studies, with Charu and the minute household issues that constitute each and every single day. He would depend more on those little homely pleasures that were abundantly and easily available; yet they retained a beauty. These were the elements that were daily touched and savoured and which nonetheless remained pristine and pure. They were the elements with which he would light up his domestic life, thus remaining enveloped in an aura of peace. The modest joys that brought about even greater joy were the essence of what Bhupati had planned for himself.

In actuality Bhupati found that simple love was not at all that simple. If what could not be readily purchased did not voluntarily come within reach, finding it elsewhere was practically an impossibility.

A loving intimate relationship with Charu appeared to be unattainable. Bhupati could only fault himself for this. He thought, 'After spending twelve years merely chasing after the newspaper, the art of conversing with my wife has been completely lost'. With evening fall Bhupati would eagerly return home and desultorily utter a word or two with Charu – who responded in like. However, continuing in this manner turned out to be impossibility. At this inability, he felt great shame. He had assumed conversing with one's wife was the easiest task of all, and yet for the foolish man it turned out to be the most difficult chore. On the brink of leaving Bhupati would say – what about a game of cards, Charu? Finding no way out Charu would agree. A lot of unmindful mistakes and the game was easily lost – there was no joy in such a win.

After a lot of thought later, one day Bhupati asked, "Should we bring Manda back? You are very lonely".

Charu flared up at Manda's name, "No, there is no need".

Bhupati smiled and was innately pleased. Those who are truly devoted to their husbands find it difficult to tolerate the proclivity of others.

After overcoming the initial and spontaneous burst of acute distaste Charu thought matters over and realised that Manda's presence might make it easier to keep Bhupati in good humour. To the mental compatibility and peace that Bhupati sought from her, she was finding it absolutely impossible to respond and it hurt her. Charu found it only too apparent that, completely disregarding everybody else, Bhupati sought all the sustenance in the world from her; however, the fact that she was totally bereft of providing it scared and gravely concerned her. How long could matters carry on in this fashion? Why couldn't Bhupati find some other refuge? Why didn't he try to set up another newspaper? So far Charu never had had to tend to Bhupati's mental well-being; he had sought no nurturing from her, looked for no happiness – never had he made Charu the focus of his entire life. All of a sudden such a demand completely bewildered her. Charu just could not gauge what Bhupati sought, what could satisfy him, and, even if she did, it was no easy task for her to solace him.

If Bhupati had gradually moved forward, perhaps the matter might not have been so difficult for Charu to accept. However, suddenly Bhupati turning a pauper and looking to her for alms shook her entire being.

Charu, "Alright then, send for Manda; looking after you will be a lot easier".

Bhupati answered with a smile, "There is really no need to take care of me in any special way".

Innately hurt he thought, 'I am a shrivelled man without any sensitivity – hence making Charu happy is impossible'.

Keeping this in mind he took recourse to literature. Friends visiting him found him engrossed in reading Tennyson, Byron or even Bankimchandra. This sudden love for literature made him the laughing stock among his friends.

One evening, after the lamps were lit, Bhupati entered the room and said a little awkwardly, "Can I read aloud something?'

"Why not?"

Finding an acute lack of enthusiasm, Bhupati was a little uncomfortable. He mustered up courage and said, "This is a summary of a poem by Tennyson ..."

But all went to waste. Much hesitation and awkwardness led Bhupati to fumble and search for the appropriate words. It was apparent from Charu's blank gaze that she was not really paying any attention. In that mildly lit room, the intimate moments of leisure did not bring any degree of fulfilment and nearness.

After a couple of more such attempts, Bhupati gave up all effort to discuss literature with his wife.

Chapter 15

After any grievous injury, just as the nerves do not recognise the agonising pain at first, Charu did not realise the searing ache at the initial pain of parting from Amal.

However, as the days went by, lack of Amal's presence and the emptiness and meaninglessness of life increased proportionately. Charu was stunned at this unexpected discovery. Thrown out of paradise, into which desert had she been suddenly cast? As each day went by, the arid wasteland only increased. She had not even been aware of this barren emptiness.

No sooner did she awake in the morning than her heart would thud violently – it was borne home to her that Amal was no longer there. In the mornings, when she sat on the verandah, incessantly her thoughts would reiterate – Amal would not turn up. Amal would not come and take his leave before going to college – there was no looking forward to hearing about new authors, new compositions, or just fun times together. There was nobody to stitch luxurious articles for or work towards fulfilling absurd demands.

Charu herself was amazed at the unbearable agony and pain she was going through. The continuing ache caused her grave concern. She continually questioned herself, "Why this unbearable agony – what relation does Amal have with me that I am putting up with so much sorrow for him? What is this that is happening to me after such a long time?"

Charu continued to question, continued to be surprised – and yet no relief was in sight. Thoughts of Amal encompassed her so thoroughly that she found no respite – neither exterior nor interior brought her any kind of reprieve.

Instead of protecting her from the onslaught of Amal's memory, the affectionate and foolish Bhupati constantly brought up memories of Amal.

Finally Charu gave up the battle with herself, accepting her own plight. Lovingly she nurtured memories of Amal in her own heart.

Matters came to such a pass that meditating and focussing on memories of Amal secretly in her own heart became the focus of Charu's existence. The greatest pride in her life was those past memories.

In the midst of the housework, Charu fixed a time – she would lock and bar the doors to her room and immerse herself on any minute memory of her times with Amal and all the moments spent in his company. She would lie face upturned on the pillow and repeat "Amal, Amal, Amal!" As if from across the seas the response would come — *What is it... what is it Bouthan?* Charu would wipe dry her tears and ask, "Why did you leave in anger, in such a manner, Amal?

I had committed no sin. Probably I would not have suffered in this fashion if you had left after bidding farewell normally". Charu would speak as though Amal was seated right in front of her. She would say, "Amal, I have not forgotten you even for a day, not even for a moment. All the best qualities of my life, you have helped to blossom. I will worship you all my life".

In this manner, Charu burrowed deep within her world and from within all the darkness built up a temple of her own sorrowful tears. There, neither her husband nor anybody else in the world had any rights whatsoever. That sanctified place was as secret as it was deep, as it was beloved. She entered therein unmasking and leaving behind all pretensions. As she left and re-entered the routine world, the mask slipped back into place and she resumed the role of laughing and going about all mundane tasks.

Chapter 16

In this manner, discarding all her turmoil and anxiety Charu found some kind of peace in the midst of her overwhelming sorrow and agony; with single-minded devotion and care she looked after her husband. When Bhupati was asleep, slowly Charu would bend low and respectfully gather the dust from his feet. Whether it was in caring, tending or any housework, she left no desire of her husband untended. Knowing that it pained her husband to see his protégées neglected in any way, Charu personally took great care to ensure that their hospitality remained vibrant and all — encompassing. Handling all responsibilities in this manner, Charu would end her day by partaking of whatever was left from Bhupati's meal.

All this tender and loving care rekindled Bhupati's youth. It appeared that he had only recently married Charu. Accoutred well, in laughter and amiability Bhupati cast aside all worries and problems. Just as appetite returns after an illness, a sensation of bodily hunger is felt, those wondrous and potent feelings were aroused. Hiding from his friends and even Charu, Bhupati began reading poetry. He thought to himself, 'After losing the newspaper and contending with innumerable problems, at last I have been able to rediscover my wife'.

Bhupati said to Charu, "Charu, why have you completely given up writing these days?"

Charu responded, "... some writing that was..."

Bhupati: "Truly, I have yet to find someone who writes as well as you amongst the modern Bengali writers of the day. What the critic said in the magazine is an exact reflection of my opinion".

Bhupati then proceeded to take out a paper and make a detailed comparison of the writing style of Charu and Amal. Snatching it away and blushing fierily, Charu rapidly hid it.

Bhupati thought to himself, "It is impossible to write unless there is a compatible partner; just have patience – I will have to put in some practice as regards writing and then Charu will be enthused into writing again".

In great secrecy Bhupati began to write into a notebook. Repeatedly consulting a dictionary and scratching out lines composed, Bhupati began to fill his spare hours. He had to put in so much effort and pain that gradually he became quite attached to these hardily won creative efforts.

Finally getting someone to make a copy, Bhupati handed in his writing to his wife saying, "One of my friends has just started writing. I know nothing of these matters – why don't you take a look and let me know what you think".

Handing Charu the notebook, Bhupati left the room with a great deal of trepidation. Charu had no difficulty at all in seeing through the wiles of the innocent Bhupati.

She read the writing and smiled at the subject matter and mode of writing. Alas, when Charu was trying so hard to worship her husband – why was he scattering the efforts asunder in this manner?

If he did not make such an effort and remained just as he was, it would have been much easier for Charu to draw close to her husband. Charu intensely desired that Bhupati did not fall below her standards in any way.

Putting aside the book, Charu stared blindly into the distance for some time. Amal too used to bring her his new writings to appraise critically.

In the evening Bhupati, in eager expectation, started examining the flowering plants on the verandah. He could not summon up the courage to ask any questions.

Charu said by herself, "Is this your friend's first effort?"

"Yes."

"It is excellent – does not seem like a first effort at all."

Thrilled Bhupati began to think, "How is it possible to bring in my own name and join it with this anonymous author..."

Bhupati's notebook began to fill-up with great speed. There would not be too much of a delay before the name was revealed.

Chapter 17

Charu would ensure that she kept track of the time when overseas letters were delivered. The first letter was from Aden; in a letter addressed to Bhupati, Amal had conveyed his respectful regards to Charu. There was also a letter from Suez in which she was once again remembered in a similar manner. From Malta it was yet again a similar story.

Charu did not receive even one letter directly from Amal. She repeatedly went through Bhupati's letter, but found no allusion to herself other than a formal expression of respect.

The melancholic tranquillity that had shrouded Charu these past couple of days was shattered at this wilful negligence. Once again her heart seemed to be torn asunder. Yet one more time a storm arose in the midst of her life and household.

Every once in a while Bhupati would wake up deep at night to find Charu not there. A search would reveal her sitting by the open window to the south. Seeing him Charu would hurriedly say, "The room is so hot, I am sitting here in the hope of a little breeze".

Gravely worried, Bhupati immediately arranged for a hand drawn fan and kept an earnest vigil on his wife's health. Charu would laugh and say, "I am fine, why do you worry unnecessarily?" She exerted all the strength she possessed to bring forth this smile.

Amal reached England. Charu had convinced herself that perhaps on the way Amal hadn't had the time or opportunity to write separately to her. On reaching, definitely a long epistle would be sent. But, there was no such lengthy letter from Amal.

Each scheduled delivery day for the mail Charu would restlessly go about her household chores and keep a watchful eye at the same time. Just in case Bhupati responded negatively, she hesitated to even enquire from him whether or not there was any letter.

Under such circumstances one morning Bhupati gently walked up to her and asked, "There is something for you – do you want to take a look?"

Startled Charu put forward her hand immediately.

Jesting, Bhupati refused to cooperate.

Impatiently, Charu tried to wrest away the desired article from him. She thought, 'From the morning my heart was telling me that there would be a letter – this can never be a mistake'. Bhupati continued to laugh even harder. He began to circle the bed to avoid Charu.

Unable to do a thing, Charu sat down abruptly, eyes swimming with tears.

Pleased at Charu's eagerness, Bhupati quickly brought out the notebook of his compositions and putting it in her lap said, "Do not be angry, here it is!"

Chapter 18

Although Amal had informed Bhupati that, thanks to the pressure of studies, he would not be able to write at length, days without any kind of communication from Amal became a virtual nightmare for Charu.

In the evening, amidst a lot of other conversations, Charu told her husband in calm disinterested tones, "Isn't it feasible to send a telegram to England and find out how Amal is keeping?"

"In a letter a fortnight ago he mentioned that studies were keeping him very busy."

"Oh! Then there is no need. I was wondering that – being in a foreign country, what if he has fallen ill ..."

"No, if it were something like that, we would have got word. Sending a telegram is no mean expense."

The expense was the final deterrent and both agreed that to refrain from sending any telegram was the best idea.

A couple of days later Charu said, "My sister is in Chinsurah now. Can you get some news of her today?"

Bhupati, "Why, is she not well?"

"No, it is not that – but you know how pleased they are when you go across."

To keep Charu's word Bhupati set off for Howrah station. On the way, the gentleman in charge of sending telegraph messages handed him a note. Perhaps Amal was ill; worriedly Bhupati opened the message to find written, "I am well."

What could this mean? Examining the message he found that it was a pre-paid response.

Bhupati did not proceed with his journey to Howrah. Returning home he handed his wife the telegram. Charu turned pale seeing it in Bhupati's hands.

An investigation clarified the matter. Charu had mortgaged her jewellery and with the money sent the telegram. Bhupati said, "I just can't understand the meaning of all this".

Bhupati quite naturally thought there was no need to have done so much. If she had only requested me a bit, I would have made the arrangements. To secretly send a servant to mortgage jewellery – that was not good.

From time to time Bhupati's mind kept questioning – why did Charu over-react in this manner? The pinpricks of a vague suspicion began to disturb him. He wanted to ignore the qualms and tried his best to do so – but the persistent pain remained.

Chapter 19

Amal was well and yet had not cared enough to write! How had such a complete severing of ties taken place? A keen desire grew in Charu to just once put across this question – but the ocean lay in between and there was no way to bridge the gap. It was a cruel parting, helpless parting – a parting beyond all redemption, beyond all questions.

Charu found it impossible to remain up and about any longer. Her work was neglected, mistakes abounded, and servants started stealing. People began gossiping noticing her plight, but Charu still paid no heed. Finally Bhupati noticed and even thought what had never occurred to him before. For him life turned to ashes.

The few days of joyous abandon he had enjoyed began to shame him. How could a man be cheated in this manner?

All that Charu had done to soothe him and shower him with affection began to chide him for being a fool.

At last, when Bhupati remembered those treasured compositions of his, he felt like sinking into the ground. Like one sharply goaded, he stormed into Charu's room and asked, "Where are those notebooks of my writing?"

"They are with me."

"Give them to me." Charu had been making some food for Bhupati and asked, "Do you need them right now?"

"Yes, immediately."

Putting down her cooking, Charu fetched all the papers from the almirah. Impatiently he snatched them from her and threw them violently into the fire.

Charu tried to retrieve them asking, "What have you done!"

Bhupati roared out, "Stop it!"

Bewildered, Charu stopped abruptly. All the writings were burnt to ashes.

Charu understood the root cause of the reaction and sighed deeply. Leaving aside the half-done cooking, she moved away.

Bhupati had not intended to destroy the writing. But, seeing the fire blazing in front, something had flared up in him too. Unable to exert self-control, and feeling like one thwarted and made a fool of, he threw the root cause of it all into the fire.

When all had turned to ashes, when Bhupati's anger had simmered down, the manner in which Charu had left burdened with the weight of her own guilt and replete with sorrow made Bhupati awake from a stupor. He looked up to find that Charu had been cooking carefully a dish that he particularly enjoyed.

Bhupati stood leaning on the railing of the verandah. He pondered on the fact that Charu slaved tirelessly only because of him. All such efforts to hoodwink him, the efforts at deception – could there be anything more pathetic in the world? Mournfully his heart cried out, "Alas, O pitiable one – there was no need for all this. All this while I was not even aware that it was not love I was receiving.

My life had passed by in proof-checking – there was no need to have gone to so much trouble."

Bhupati then distanced Charu's life from his own and began to observe her from a distance, much in the same manner as a doctor observes a patient. There was no place she could go to, there was none she could confide in. That feeble feminine heart had been so thoroughly overwhelmed by life all around. There was none to whom she could confide her all and nowhere to lay bare her heart. Yet she had to go about all her household chores and behave in accordance with a mundane routine – just like any other ordinary man or woman.

Returning to his bedroom Bhupati found Charu standing by the window, staring blindly through the open window. He stood by her and, not saying a word, in silence gently patted her on the head.

Chapter 20

Friends enquired of Bhupati – "What is the matter, why do you keep so busy?"

"Newspaper, you understand ..."

"Newspaper yet again? Will you then have to give up even your ancestral property for this newspaper?"

"No, this is not my own ..."

"Then?"

"A newspaper is to be published in Mysore – they have appointed me editor."

"You will leave all behind and travel to Mysore? You are taking Charu with you?"

"No, my uncles will be shifting here."

"This passion for editing will never leave you."

Bhupati only remarked, "In every life there has to be a passion of some kind".

At the moment of parting Charu asked, "When will you return?"

"If you feel alone, let me know and I will come."

Just as he was about to leave, Charu suddenly ran up to the door and clutching his hand firmly pleaded, "Take me with you, don't leave me behind here".

Bhupati abruptly stopped. Charu's grip slackened and fell loose. Bhupati moved away and stood on the verandah.

It was clear to Bhupati that Charu wanted to escape the searing memories of severing ties with Amal that lingered in the house. – 'But, did she not think of me even once? Where is my escape? Even away from my native land, will I not be able to forget a wife who is constantly dreaming of another? Every companionless, friendless evening I will have to give her company? Each evening, when, I return, the time I am forced to spend with a woman in mourning will become a terrifying nightmare. A woman who is dead inside – how long can I carry her burden? How many more years will I have to survive in this manner! The house that has been razed to the ground – can I not discard the bricks, will I have to continue to bear them about?'

Bhupati answered, "No, that is not possible".

In a flash all the blood drained from Charu's face, leaving her pale; she gripped the bed firmly with her both hands.

Instantly Bhupati said, "Come Charu, accompany me".

Charu's only response was, "No, let it be".

Streer Patra
(The Wife's Epistle)

Respected Husband,

Humble offerings at your lotus-feet.

Though it has been fifteen years since we have been married, I have not yet written a letter to you. Forever I have been with you – you have heard me speak a lot and I too have heard you talk, never has there been any gap and opportune moment to write to you.

Now I am on a pilgrimage to Srikshetra and you are going about your usual office work. Your bonding with Kolkata is akin to that of a snail with its shell, being irreversibly attached to your body and mind. That is surely the only reason why you did not apply for leave from your office. Probably that was what Providence intended; He sanctioned my leave application.

I am the second daughter-in-law of your family. Today, at the end of fifteen years, I have just come to realise that besides this, I also have another relationship with the Almighty and my world. That is the sole reason why I am attempting to communicate with you; it is not the daughter-in-law of your family who is writing today.

When the Almighty had ordained what would be my relationship with you people, besides Him, none knew of the possibility. During that childhood my brother and I were both afflicted with enteric fever. He died, I survived. All women of the neighbourhood said, 'Since Mrinal is a girl, she lived, had she been a man would she had been spared!' Yama (the God of Death) is skilled in the art of stealing; it is precious objects which attract his attention.

Death is not for me – and to explain that sordid fact at length is the prime purpose behind this letter to you.

When a distant relative accompanied your friend Nirod in choosing a prospective bride, I was merely twelve years old. Our home was in a remote village, there jackals could be heard even during the day! It was a long and arduous journey to our village. What a lot of trouble you all had been put to that day – and then there was our regional cooking; jocular remarks are made about it even today.

Your mother was determined to compensate for the lack of looks of the eldest daughter-in-law by bringing in the second daughter-in-law who was a ravishing beauty. Or else why would all of you have taken so much trouble to travel to our village?

In Bengal one does not have to go in search of a bride – the choices come pressing down on you and it becomes difficult to get away.

My father was tense and scared and my mother prayed to the Almighty. The daughter's beauty was all the capital she had to propitiate the urban God. But, the daughter herself remained unaware and whatever price was paid would be accepted. That is why no matter how beautiful or talented, the diffidence never completely vanished.

This panic of not just the family, but the entire village pressed down heavily on me. All the light in the firmament that day and all the strength in the universe appeared to firmly stand guard to a twelve-year old village girl and ensure her passing a vital examination – there was no place anywhere for me to hide.

The flutes resounded, as if making the skies weep, and thus I entered your household. Despite thoroughly examining all my flaws, all in the neighbourhood were forced to admit that I could truly be regarded as beautiful. My elder sister-in-law grew grim at that; but I wonder, of what use was that beauty to me? If creation of the object called beauty with the mud of the holy Ganges had been the idea of some learned man of in the past, it might have been worthy of appreciation. But it was a creation of Providence, for his own pleasure. Hence in a family of your ilk it had no worth.

It did not take all of you very long to forget about my beauty. But, you all were forced to accept and remember at every step that I was also intelligent. It came to me so naturally that even after spending all these years in your household, it still remains intact! My mother was extremely concerned because of this very factor – she considered intelligence as a bane for women. If a person who had to accept restrictions instead sought to follow the norms of intelligence, she was bound to be lacerated and broken in no time. But, tell me, what could I do? Sheer oversight made the Almighty give me far more intelligence than was required for a bride belonging to your household – to whom could I possibly return it? You all had abused me all the time as being very much of an upstart – abuses are a sign of weaklings and hence I forgive you.

One quality of mine about which all of you remained unaware was my ability to compose poetry. I would do so in secret. Good, bad, indifferent, no matter what, it did not have a barricade put up all around. That was my freedom and that was where I was I. Whatever quality of mine did not fit your concept of the second daughter-in-law you all neither liked, nor recognised. That I am a poet, you all did not even come to know in the course of these fifteen years.

The memory of your household that most strongly comes to mind is the image of the cowshed. It is located just beside the stairs leading to the inner sanctum – besides the open courtyard in front they have no place where they can wander about, chewing cud at leisure. At one corner of the courtyard, in a large wooden bowl their feed would be put out. In the morning the bearer was kept very busy; the hungry animals would spend all the time till then licking the sides of the wooden tumbler till the wood almost splintered. I am a village girl – the day I newly came to your home, the two cows and three calves seemed the only familiar relatives. As long as I remained a new bride, before my own meal, I would feed them.

When I grew up a little and my attachment to these animals became an open secret, there was a lot of laughter and questions raised about my lineage.

My daughter died as soon as she was born. She had beckoned me to join her at the time. If she had lived, she would have been whatever was major in my life, whatever was the truth, she would have brought everything; instead of merely the second daughter-in-law I would have become a mother. A mother, even living in a family belongs to the entire world. I bore the pain and agony of becoming a mother, but could not savour the freedom of motherhood.

I remember the English doctor had been amazed at seeing our inner sanctum and had been just as irritated at seeing the maternity room, soundly scolding all of you. You have a little garden in front and there is no dearth of furniture or decorative pieces all over the house. But the inner sanctum is like the reverse side of a beautiful embroidered article. No care is taken, there is no pride, and there is virtually no beauty either – dim lights flicker; the wind slinks in like a thief; the dirt on the courtyard refuses to budge; the stains on the walls and on the floors remain indelible. But the doctor had made a mistake; he thought that all this caused us continual grief. It was just the opposite; neglect is like the ash that smothers the fire within, but the heat is not apparent from outside. When self-respect diminishes, neglect no longer appears unfair, hence there is no pain. That is why women have an innate awkwardness even in feeling sorrow and pain. So I say, if your intention is to ensure that women have to have sadness thrust on them, then as far as possible it is better to neglect them. With affection the pain of sadness only increases manifold.

It never occurred to me to brood on the fact that no matter how you keep me, there is bound to be sorrow. When delivering our child, death was at the fore – even then there was no question of fright. What does life hold that we have to be afraid of death? Those who have been nurtured with love and care – they are the ones who find death painful. If death had beckoned me that day, I would have gone with him, as easily as uprooted clumps of grass are pulled out.

A woman of Bengal wants to embrace death every moment. But, what is particularly brave to die in such a manner? We are even ashamed to die – death is that easy for us.

Like the evening star my daughter appeared briefly in the firmament and then disappeared. Once again it was back to the routine of attending to my daily chores and the cattle. Life would have continued in much the same fashion and there would have been no need at all to write to you. But the most minute seed blown by the wind nestles in between the crevices of the wall and is responsible for its ultimate destruction. Amidst the concrete arrangements of my life and family a small spark from somewhere nestled in my heart and it is from that point that the cracks began to appear.

After the death of her widowed mother, my elder sister-in-law's sister took shelter in our household. Thanks to her cousin's persecution, all of you must have thought – what a nuisance. It is my unfortunate habit that led me to support her wholeheartedly – finding her helpless and unwanted. It was, after all, an insult to be forced to accept the shelter and hospitality in the household of another. How was it possible to turn away one who had no choice but to accept this humiliation and insult.

Then there was my sister-in-law's plight to think about. Out of pity she had given shelter to her sister. But her husband's reluctance forced her to playact in a manner that depicted bare tolerance of her sister's presence. There was no way she could openly express her affection – after all, she was primarily a devout wife.

My heart grew even heavier at this situation. My elder sister-in-law engaged the orphaned girl in all manner of servile duties, I felt ashamed and sorry. She was extremely anxious to prove that Bindu's presence to the family was in actuality a great convenience – she put in a lot of work, but was cheap at the price.

Besides a lofty paternal lineage, my sister-in-law had nothing much to speak by way of beauty or wealth. It is by maintaining a distance and keeping herself withdrawn and occupying as little space as possible that she remained in our house. It is a matter of common knowledge how my father-in-law was persuaded by dint of begging and pleading to take her into his family as a bride. She always regarded her marriage in this family as a great offence.

But, this sagacious attitude was causing me no end of problems. I could not demean myself. It is not in me to propagate as bad what my heart dictates is good. You too have plenty of proof of that yourself.

I dragged Bindu to my room. Didi, the elder sister-in-law, said, "This daughter-in-law is now going to spoil a girl belonging to a poor family". She complained that I was beckoning grave danger closer. However, I am quite sure that actually she was greatly relieved because now all the fault could be directed my way. The affection that she dared not show could now be showered on Bindu, thereby relieving her of the burden. Though my sister-in-law tried to prove how young Bindu was, there is no doubt that she was older than fourteen. You know that she was so unappealing that if she fell and broke her head, people around would be concerned more about the condition of the floor. Further, being an orphan, there was none to marry her off and nobody was courageous enough to voluntarily do so either.

Bindu approached me with great trepidation, as if her touch would sully. In the whole wide world there appeared to be not a corner for her to be born and she spent all her time avoiding people and evading them as best as she could. Her step-brother did not leave her an iota of room; there might be room for offal and rubbish, simply because people did not remember them. But even this was not to be for Bindu.

When I called Bindu to my room, she could barely accept that there was actually a little space for her there. But my task became that much more difficult because she came out in virulent red spots, which you suspected to be chicken pox. After all, she was Bindu. Before arrangements could be made to secretly send her for treatment, the spots subsided completely – making the situation even more suspect. After all, she was Bindu.

One big advantage about being unwanted is that even death and sickness bypasses one. The disease did not affect her, but it was only too apparent that to shelter the unwanted was the most difficult task of all. The more one needed shelter, the more difficult it was to get.

Once Bindu got over her fright of me, another major problem developed. She became so attached that I was afraid. Such a display of emotion has never been witnessed before. Her thirst for gazing at me could not be quenched; she would help me to dress and, in short, became totally obsessed with me.

There is no space at all in your inner sanctum. To the north of the boundary wall, the colour of the leaves of the fruit tree turning a bright red indicated to me that Spring was drawing close. That the heart of the young girl in my household would similarly blossom I had no idea. Bindu's love and affection hounded me; but, at the same time, it must be admitted that reflected in this love I found a true image of myself that I had never ever seen before in life. That was my true image of freedom.

On the other hand, that I was taking care of someone like Bindu caused a positive furore in my household. There was no end to the bickering and verbal skirmishes. The day a piece of jewellery was stolen from my room, none of you hesitated to accuse her. When there were raids in the house because of suspected freedom fighters – it was immediately suspected that Bindu was a female agent; the reason for this suspicion was simple – after all, she was Bindu.

All the maids and servants in your household objected violently to any chore they had to do for her. Bindu herself would shrink in embarrassed shame too. It is because of all these reasons that my expenses as regards Bindu spiralled upwards. A separate maidservant had to be engaged. You were so angry at the clothes I bought her that you stopped giving me pocket money. I too took to wearing coarse linen and would wash my own dishes – a sight which you did not appreciate at all. What I did-not understand then and still do not understand is that – my displeasure was not necessary to heed; but if you were unhappy, it was just not acceptable.

Just as your anger increased over the years, so too did Bindu grow. This natural process embarrassed you all much – the reason escapes me altogether. I am amazed as to why you all did not actually turn her away from your household. I am quite aware of the fact that you are afraid of me and definitely in awe of my innate intelligence.

Not leaving on her own steam, Bindu's departure was finally arranged by fixing a matrimonial alliance for her. My elder sister-in-law expressed great relief that the honour of the family would be maintained. What sort of person the groom was I did not know – but I consoled Bindu saying, "Don't worry, I have heard that he is a good man". Though she begged and pleaded even I could not summon up the courage to ask for her marriage to be cancelled. Just five days before the wedding she pleaded for death; honestly speaking, if there were any easy way out that might have been the easiest solution for her. My sister-in-law shed hidden tears, just as she had the day Bindu had arrived. But, there was no option, Bindu would have to marry. I had wanted Bindu to be married from our house, but the groom insisted otherwise – that was apparently their family tradition. I dressed Bindu with some of my jewellery; my sister-in-law noticed but chose to ignore – do forgive her for this offence, please.

It turned out that Bindu's husband was a lunatic and had been forcibly married off. The fact was not obvious and it was only sometimes that he turned violent and had to be locked up. The day of the marriage such facts had been kept a secret – truly, it was women who were the worst enemy of their own gender. After marriage the first day he was fine, but, with all the excitement, the sickness flared up the second day and he had to be physically restrained. On the third day, Bindu was asked to join her husband on their marital bed; he was calm, but terrified of her mother-in-law's wrath and the circumstances she found herself in, Bindu found it impossible to say a word. Only when he fell asleep did she manage to make her escape.

My entire body burnt in anger. I emphasised that this was no marriage and suggested that legal recourse be taken. All the family shrugged off the entire responsibility of her marrying a mad man. In the meanwhile, Bindu's in-laws came to fetch her back and set up a big commotion. If even a dumb animal sought shelter from the slaughter house, I would never deliver it back to be killed. It was the same with Bindu. I refused to send her back and said that the in-laws could go right ahead and file a report if they so desired. A lot was said to persuade Bindu to return – after all, no matter what, he was her husband and it was her duty to fulfil wifely commitments! But neither any religious dictum nor any social norm could persuade me to let go of my firm convictions.

I was sure that, if sent back, Bindu would never return to our house. Suddenly I remembered my brother Sarat – he was involved in a lot of social activities and might be just the person to help Bindu. I was explaining all these matters to him, when you suddenly entered the room, asking, "What new problem have you cooked up now?" You asked if I had hidden Bindu anywhere. I answered that if she had returned, I might have done so, but not to worry, that was a course of action she would never think of undertaking.

You did not like to see Sarat because the police might be keeping an eye on him for political complications. I heard from you that Bindu had run away again – Sarat immediately left to find out the facts of the matter. He returned in the evening with the news that where Bindu had sought shelter, she had been delivered back to her in-laws – who found it impossible to forget the fact that they had been put to no little expense for not just getting news of her, but also apprehending her and bringing her back.

At this juncture an aunt arrived en route to a pilgrimage and I suggested accompanying her. All of you were very happy that my thoughts had turned to religion and agreed; it might be the perfect solution and avoid my getting involved in Bindu's imbroglio. As a matter of fact, all of you were so relieved that none remembered that I might cause even greater complications by getting involved with Bindu even from Kolkata. Wednesday was the day of departure – and all this was decided on Sunday. I sent for Sarat and said, "Somehow or the other, Bindu will have to be put on the train for Puri on Wednesday".

Sarat happily agreed. However, that evening he came looking grave. On asking if there were any problems, he said that there was no need for any further intervention – Bindu had committed suicide by setting herself on fire. She had left a note for me, which they had destroyed.

The entire country rose in anger – dying in this manner had apparently become fashionable. There were so many other means she could have adopted – neither did she make any impact while she lived and of course her death was equally nondescript.

I left on a pilgrimage – there was a need for it, though for Bindu it had held no further meaning.

Looking back for me there was no sorrow as such in your household. There was food; no matter what your brother's character was – there is nothing that I can blame you for. But, despite it all, there is no way I will ever return to your house – I have seen and felt Bindu's plight. I have come to realise what identity a woman has. It has been my observation that no matter how much force you of the so-called society apply, there is an end to it – death is far greater than any of you. Bindu no longer is a mere Bengali girl, her brother's sister et al. Where she has gone, she has an unsurpassable unique identity.

This girl's death pierced my broken heart and I asked the Almighty: Why is it that what is the most petty is the most hard too. Why was I unable to cross this threshold even for a split second? But when death sounded his bugle, it takes no time for all masks to be torn asunder.

No longer do I have any fear of your narrow, petty world. For an instance Bindu had penetrated the shield and shown me what lay beyond. Today I emerge to find – there is no place to rest my ego. Whoever has found appealing this unadorned form of mine — has seen me in the background of the beautiful firmament. This is where your wife has died.

You think I am going to die? No, that old jest I will not spring on you. Mirabai, too, was a woman like me and her shackles of convention were just as heavy. But, in order to live she did not have to die.

It is this staunch adherence which remains and lives.

I too will live.

But I am no longer your footstalk.

Footloose
Mrinal